VIOLA S.WAMP is WATCHING YOU

W9-BRM-549

WITH YOU AND WITHOUT YOU

Other books by
ANN M. MARTIN

ANN M. MARTIN

WITH YOU AND WITHOUT YOU

AN
APPLE
PAPERBACK

SCHOLASTIC INC.
New York Toronto London Auckland Sydney

The author would like to thank DR. ERIC J. EICHHORN, cardiologist, for his sensitive evaluation of the manuscript.

No part of this publication may be reproduced in whole or in part, or stored in a retrieval system, or transmitted in any form or by any means, electronic, mechanical, photocopying, recording, or otherwise, without written permission of the publisher. For information regarding permission, write to Holiday House, 18 East 53rd Street, New York, NY 10022.

ISBN 0-590-43625-2

Copyright © 1986 by Ann M. Martin. All rights reserved. Published by Scholastic Inc., 730 Broadway, New York, NY 10003, by arrangement with Holiday House, Inc. APPLE PAPERBACKS is a registered trademark of Scholastic Inc.

12 11 10 9 8 7 6 5 4   1 2 3 4 5/9

Printed in the U.S.A.   23

This book is for
CLAUDIA WERNER,
for all the years.

WITH YOU AND WITHOUT YOU

Contents

BOOK I

Autumn

Chapter One

November 12 was not the greatest day in my life. I plodded home from school that afternoon thinking about a piece of bad news I'd received: my English teacher had announced that our class was going to participate in a winter pageant before Christmas vacation. I wasn't sure what a winter pageant would involve, but I didn't like the sound of it. I would probably have to do something on a stage before an audience, and that was worrying me.

I was also worried about my father. He'd been very tired lately, and ever since last summer he'd been getting short of breath. Sometimes his legs would swell up. So he was going to visit our family doctor that afternoon. It was his second visit in a week. But since Dad was usually as healthy as a horse, the idea of having to be a snowflake or a surgarplum was more on my mind.

The day was bitterly cold. We were in for a hard winter according to *The Farmer's Almanac,* and also according to my four-year-old sister, Hope, who had spent a lot of time studying the stripes on the woolly bears. The stripes were very wide, and Hope's day-care center teachers said the wider the stripe, the harder the winter.

I pulled my scarf tighter, lowered my head against the wind, and quickened my pace. The sky was steely gray, that harsh, sharp sort of gray you find sometimes in the eyes of German shepherds. It was a color I disliked.

I turned the corner onto Bayberry and hurried by the Hansons' house on the corner with its untidy yard and the dogs whining in their pen. Then I hurried by the Whites' immaculate house and waved to Susie and Mandy, Hope's friends, who were trying to jump rope, but who were so bundled up they could hardly move. The Petersens' home was next (my best friend, Denise, lived there), then came the Washburns', and across from their house was 25 Bayberry Street. I always approached our house from the other side of the road so I could get the fullest view of it. I stood in front of the Washburns' for a few seconds, just looking.

Our house was very special to me. It was the biggest and oldest house on Bayberry Street, and generations of us O'Haras had lived in it. It had been in our family ever since it was built, almost two hundred years ago. The house grinned a welcome to me. I noticed that someone, probably Mom, had hung a bunch of dried

corn on the front door that morning—a sure sign of
Thanksgiving and the holiday season. The corn would
stay up until it was time for the Christmas wreath. I
smiled, feeling momentarily satisfied and excited, and
took off across the street in a run.

I ran all the way up the lawn to the porch and leaped
up the four steps in two bounds. Then I slipped the
house key from around my neck and let myself in.

"Hello?" I called, slamming the door behind me.

No answer. I was the first one home. Some days I
liked the peace and quiet, some days I didn't. That
day, feeling uneasy about the pageant, I longed for a
little company, my sister Carrie's in particular.

I was what my mother and father called a latchkey
kid. Brent, my brother, and Carrie were latchkey kids,
too. Our parents both worked, and we three older kids
were on our own from three o'clock, when school let
out, until six or so when our parents came home. Hope
was not a latchkey kid. She was too little, and Mom
and Dad didn't want her to be a burden on her sisters
or brother. That was how she wound up in day care.

Every weekday morning at seven forty-five sharp,
Mom or Dad or sometimes Brent, now that he could
drive, would drop Hopie off at the Harper Early Childhood Center, a fancy day-care operation where Hope
remained under the watchful eyes of Mrs. Annette
Harper and three capable teachers until someone
picked her up in the evening.

All us O'Haras called the HECC "Hope's school,"
and Hopie felt very proud that she went to school all

day just like Brent and Carrie and I did. None of the
other little kids on Bayberry Street could claim that.

There were two reasons why both of my parents
worked. One, they enjoyed it, and two, we needed the
money. Not that we were struggling or anything. In
fact, we had plenty of money. But believe me, we
needed plenty of money for the upkeep of our big, old
house and its three and a half acres. In a house as old
as ours, something was always breaking or on the verge
of breaking, usually in one of three areas—the base-
ment, the kitchen, or a bathroom. Then, too, Mom and
Dad were facing four college educations, and Brent's
would start in less than two years.

So Mom and Dad worked. My mother was the head
of the English department at the Covington Public
School System. We lived in Neuport, Connecticut, and
Covington was the next town over. Mom had decided
years ago that she would be wise to head up the English department of a school system her children were
not a part of.

My father was an account executive at a hotshot ad-
vertising firm in New York City. He commuted there
on the train every day. Dad handled accounts like Cal-
vin Klein jeans and Chanel perfume. When I was little,
before I developed stage fright, I used to beg him to
put me in the commercials for his products. Now I
understand that he didn't have any control over that
sort of thing.

I hung up my ski jacket, put away my scarf and
mittens, set my school books on the dining room table,

and got two brownies out of the cake tin.

I opened the refrigerator and stood in front of it, looking at all the pots and plastic containers and mysterious foil-wrapped packages, and tried to figure out what to fix for dinner. Brent and Carrie and I were in charge of dinner on weekdays since we got home earlier than Mom or Dad. I decided on broccoli, potatoes in their jackets (a favorite of Hopie's), and baked chicken legs. I closed the refrigerator. Everything could be started later.

I was about to crack my math book when I heard a scratching at the back door. It was Fifi, begging to come in. I could hear her whining as I unlatched the door.

"Feef!" I cried as she bounded in, bringing a gust of frosty air with her. "You must be freezing."

"Woof!" she agreed happily, standing on her hind legs to kiss my face.

Despite her name, Fifi is not little and is not a poodle. She's a gorgeous golden retriever. Brent got her for his birthday six years ago. At the time, he thought naming her Fifi was hysterical. Now it's just embarrassing, but there's no changing a dog's name. Fifi would never answer to anything but Fifi.

Fifi trotted after me as I headed for the cabinet where her kibbles and chow and the cat food were stored. She looked happy and smug, probably thinking, *I knew she'd give in*.

I gave her a biscuit shaped like a mailman, and she took it delicately between her teeth and, without being told, settled down in the kitchen to eat it. An O'Hara rule is that all pets must be fed on linoleum. It's awfully hard to get crunchies out of a shag rug.

I whistled for Charlie and Mouse, our cats, but my sister Carrie came into the kitchen instead.

"Hi!" I greeted her. "You're home late today."

"I know," she replied. She began rummaging through the refrigerator before she even took off her coat. "The bus had a flat tire. It took forever to get it fixed." Carrie carefully set an apple on the kitchen counter, then hung her coat in the closet and put her books on the bench in the back hall.

Carrie sat at the kitchen table taking tiny, neat bites out of her apple. She was ten, two years younger than I, and in her last year at Neuport Elementary School. Although Carrie and I are the closest in age of us four kids, we couldn't look more different. I have olive skin and brown hair with hazel eyes (the same as Mom and Hopie), and Carrie has fair skin with hair so dark it's almost black, and deep brown eyes (the same as Dad and Brent). Carrie has a heart-shaped face, while mine is long and thin. Also, Carrie is petite, while I am tall for my age, so that she looks much younger than her age, and I look older than mine.

I poured another glass of juice and sat down across from her. "So?" I said.

"So?" she countered.

"Anything exciting happen today?"

"Tricia Kennedy barfed in gym class."

"That's not exciting, that's gross."

"It was exciting for the nurse. Tricia barfed all the way down the hall and into the nurse's office and all over the—"

"Carrie! That's disgusting."

"Okay, okay. Did anything exciting happen to you?" I sighed.

"What?" Carrie crunched loudly on her apple.

"Mr. Landi announced that we're going to be in a pageant this Christmas."

"Ohhhh," said Carrie knowingly, probably remembering last spring when I fainted the morning I had to give an oral report for my social studies class. "Do you have to be in it?"

"Well, Mr. Landi hasn't given us many details yet, but you know how he is. Mr. Participation."

Carrie nodded. After a few moments she asked, "Are you having auditions or what?"

"I guess," I said.

"So be absent the day of the auditions. Tell Mom you think you're getting the virus back again."

"Carrie, you're a genius!" I cried. Last spring I'd gotten a virus that I couldn't shake. It stayed with me for months, and I'd been hot and achy and irritable all summer, and in fact until just a month or so ago. Now we were wondering if possibly Dad had the same thing, or some form of it, and nobody wanted to put up with his moaning and complaining when they'd just gotten over mine. Anyway, if I told Mom I felt it coming on again, I could probably get away with at least two days in bed.

Carrie smiled smugly at me.

"But wait," I said. "Maybe it would be worse if I stayed home. What if Mr. Landi cast me in some gigantic role? I wouldn't be able to defend myself."

"Yeah." Carrie looked thoughtful.

The two of us sat and schemed so long and so intently that Brent scared us out of our wits when he banged through the back door, Charlie and Mouse frisking ahead of him.

We jumped a mile.

"Brent!" Carrie shrieked.

"What's wrong? You look like you saw a ghost. Your hair's standing on end."

"It is not," said Carrie, but she patted her hair, checking, when she thought Brent and I weren't looking.

"Geez, she's gullible," muttered Brent from within the refrigerator. He emerged with a carton of milk.

"Well, you egg her on," I complained. "And don't drink that out of the container. Get a glass."

Brent got a glass and sat down at the kitchen table.

Carrie sat across from him dejectedly. Sometimes she has a hard time being the middle sister. She's mature enough so that Hope and I *both* look up to her, yet young enough to be pretty gullible at times. Brent has a real knack for getting under her skin.

Mouse and Charlie twined themselves lovingly around my ankles, reminding me that it was almost their dinner time. I picked Charlie up and cradled him in my arms, listening to his rumbly purrs.

Charlie was my special cat, a ginger-colored tiger.

In fact, he was everybody's favorite, except Hope's, since Mouse wasn't very loving. For some reason, Hope particularly liked Mouse. Anyway, I found Charlie two years ago. He was a tiny lost stray, mewing weakly inside a cardboard box. Someone had dumped him by the side of the road. So I brought him home and we kept him. It was as simple as that.

I gave Charlie a kiss on his furry orange face and set him on the floor with Mouse. "Carrie," I said, "why don't you feed the animals? Brent and I will start dinner. Does anyone know what time Dad's doctor's appointment is? Maybe he'll be home early."

"Don't know," said Brent vaguely. He swallowed the last of his milk.

I checked my watch. Almost five. Everyone would be home in a little over an hour. I put the chicken in the oven and washed the broccoli, while Brent scrubbed the potatoes and stuck them in a pan on the rack below the chicken. Carrie fed Fifi, Charlie, and Mouse. Then we sat at the dining room table and started our homework. We made a warm, peaceful, late-autumn scene, and I began to relax and forget about the winter pageant.

It was five forty-five when the phone rang in the kitchen.

"I'll get it!" yelled Carrie, but I beat her to it. I was hoping it was Denise Petersen, home from her piano lesson. She wasn't in my class, and I wanted to tell her about Mr. Landi and the pageant.

"Hi," I said expectantly when I picked up the phone.

"Liza?" asked the voice on the other end.

"Oh, Mom," I said, embarrassed. "Sorry. I thought you were going to be Denise. Do you have to work late tonight?" That was her usual reason for calling at this hour.

"Nooo..." she replied slowly. "I'm...at Dr. Seitz's office with Dad. He's..." (another long pause) "...still looking at your father. Running a bit late. Would you ask Brent to pick up Hope now? Dad and I won't be home for awhile."

"Is something wrong?"

"Just a little delay," said Mom.

"Mo-om."

"Liza, what is it?" asked Brent. He was standing behind me and must have been listening to my end of the conversation.

"Talk to Mom," I said, thrusting the phone at him. I crossed my arms and leaned against the kitchen table.

Brent's end of the conversation went like this:

"Mom? Hi. What's up?...Several *hours*?...Sure. I'll get Hopie. We started dinner.... You don't? We could warm it up for you later....Oh, okay. Everything all right?...Oh....Oh....Okay. See you. 'Bye."

I pounced on Brent as soon as the phone was back in its cradle. "What'd she say?"

"For us not to worry and for me to pick up Hopie." Brent grinned. He's almost a year older than most of the juniors at Neuport High and gets a big kick out of being able to drive already. "And for us to go ahead and eat, and not to save dinner for them."

"Is that *every*thing?" I pressed.

"Liza." Brent fixed his brown eyes sternly on me.

"Okay, okay." I know when to give in.

"Anyone want to come with me to get Hopie?" asked Brent with forced cheerfulness.

"Me!" cried Carrie, dashing into the kitchen.

I was pretty sure she'd heard every word Brent and I had said during the last few minutes, but she didn't ask one question, at least not before she and Brent left.

It wasn't until I was standing alone in the dark, empty front hall of 25 Bayberry, watching the headlights of our Toyota carefully inch their way backward down the long driveway, that I began to wonder why Mom was *with* Dad at Dr. Seitz's. She never left her office before six o'clock, not unless there was an emergency or a matter of extreme importance. Besides, since when did Mom go with Dad to the doctor? She didn't even go with Brent or me anymore.

Something was wrong. I could feel it.

Something was very wrong.

Chapter Two

When Hope arrived home that evening, Brent and Carrie and I didn't even tell her where Mom and Dad were, just that they were out. Hope wasn't suspicious. Her parents went out often, and her big brother and sisters baby-sat for her often. Besides, she was all wound up about school.

While Brent parked the car in the garage, Hopie ran in the back door and found me in the kitchen. She grabbed me around my knees, and craned her neck back to look up at me.

"Hi, Liza!" she cried joyously.

"Hiya, Sissy," I said, leaning over to kiss the top of her head.

Hope has a variety of nicknames—Sissy, Tink (for Tinker Bell, Hope's favorite *Peter Pan* character), and Emmy. (Emmy is short for Emily, which is actually Hope's first name. Dad is the only one who calls her

Emmy, though. It's his special name for her, since Emily was the name of his favorite grandmother.)

"Guess what," said Hope, wriggling with excitement.

"What?" I bent down to unzip her jacket.

"We made snowmen today. Not real ones, cotton ball ones. I had to leave mine at school to dry. But I made a picture of a snowman, too. Carrie has it."

Carrie came into the kitchen carrying a big piece of paper which had been rolled up and fastened with a rubber band.

"Let's see," I said.

We opened it up and spread it on the kitchen table.

It was hard to make out, since Hopie had used white paint on white paper, but sure enough, there was a wobbly snowman with stick arms and a great big red hat.

"Wow, Sissy, that's pretty," said Carrie encouragingly.

"It certainly is. I think we should put it up so everyone can see it."

"Oh, goody," said Hopie. "I'll get the tape."

We gave the snowman a place of honor on the refrigerator. Hopie chattered on and on about school. They'd taken a walk to the playground, they'd made their own play dough out of salt and water and flour, they'd learned a song about a teapot.

By the time we sat down to dinner, Hope was running out of things to say. Brent and Carrie and I tried to keep a conversation going, but we were struggling.

I'm not sure that Hope noticed anything was wrong. She was so delighted with her potato in its jacket, and had to concentrate so hard in order to eat her chicken leg, that she didn't pay much attention to the rest of us.

After dinner, nobody felt like doing anything except watching TV. That suited Hopie. She found a rerun of "Love Boat," curled up in my lap, stuck her thumb in her mouth, and was as happy as a clam.

The minutes dragged by. Seven o'clock, seven-fifteen, seven-thirty... eight-fifteen.

It had been two and a half hours since Mom called. What were Mom and Dad doing at the doctor's at 8:15 P.M.? Doctors' offices weren't even *open* at 8:15.

It was eight-thirty when we heard a car pull into the garage.

Brent and I looked at each other. Then we all looked at the back door, waiting for someone to come in.

As soon as the door opened, Hopie hurtled herself across the room and into Mom's arms.

"Mommy! We made snowmen! We made our own play dough! We went to the park!" She paused. She watched Mom close the door behind her. "Where's Daddy?" she asked.

"Just a second, Hopie," said Mom. "Let me hang my coat up. Carrie, will you please turn off the television? I want to talk to the four of you."

Something like an ice cube settled into the pit of my stomach.

"Come here, Sissy," I said.

Hope crawled back in my lap. Suddenly she knew something was wrong, too. She put her thumb in her mouth and sucked away furiously.

Brent sat down on one side of me, Carrie on the other. We were lined up on the couch as if we were waiting for a firing squad. Mom took up a position in an armchair across from us.

I giggled nervously.

Mom didn't mince any words. That wasn't her style.

"Well," she began, looking at her hands, which were in her lap, "as I'm sure you've guessed, I have some bad news. Your father is in the hospital."

"The hospital!" I cried.

Brent silenced me with a touch on my arm.

But I couldn't help crying out. I was just so surprised. How could Dad suddenly be *that* sick? I'd seen him when he left for work in the morning. He'd looked all right.

"The doctor thinks your father has heart disease," said Mom.

"How serious is it?" asked Brent.

"They're not sure right now," replied Mom. "Dr. Seitz called in a specialist tonight, a cardiologist. He's running tests. We'll have the results of some of them tomorrow. That's mostly why Dad is in the hospital now—for tests."

"How does he feel?" I asked.

"Not bad," said Mom. "Just tired, out of breath. You know how run-down he's been lately. And his legs are bothering him. They're swollen again."

I nodded.

"I'm going to pack a bag for your father and go back to the hospital. I don't know what time I'll be home tonight. Brent, you're in charge while I'm gone."

"Okay," said Brent.

"And I don't want anyone giving Brent any trouble. Here are your bedtimes, so there will be nothing to argue about: Hope, as soon as you're ready; Carrie, nine-thirty; Liza, ten o'clock; Brent, by eleven o'clock. Got that, everybody?"

We nodded grimly.

Mom went upstairs to get Dad's overnight bag.

I glanced at Brent and Carrie on either side of me. "Well?" I said.

"You know, they're making great strides in medicine and cardiology," said Brent. "We're learning about it in that special pre-med class I'm taking this year."

Brent is really smart. He's always being chosen to participate in new programs and accelerated classes.

"You wouldn't believe it," he went on. "Doctors can do all kinds of surgery these days. Coronary bypass operations are practically routine, and more and more people are surviving heart transplants. Dad could even be the next guy to get an artificial heart."

"Oh, great," I said. "The new William Schroeder. That means Dad has just *days* and *days* ahead of him. Terrific."

We fell silent. Nobody moved from the couch. Hope lay back against me, sucking her thumb and twisting her hair. The only sound in the room was Hopie slurping away.

Suddenly Carrie turned to her viciously. "Would you cut that out?" She yanked Hope's thumb out of her mouth. "What a baby."

Hope made a feeble attempt to slap Carrie's hand. Then she burst into tears.

I turned on Carrie and gave her a look that could have killed a snake. Carrie folded her arms and slumped so far down that she almost slid off the couch.

I got to my feet and picked Hopie up. She laid her head on my shoulder, crying silently. "Okay, Sissy. I'll take you upstairs to bed. It's been a long day," I said.

I left Brent and Carrie sitting at opposite ends of the couch. Just sitting. Neither one moved. Neither one said good night to Hopie.

I carried Hope through the living room and started up the stairs. She was as limp and as heavy as a sack of potatoes. She must have been dead tired.

I met my mother on her way downstairs with Dad's bag. Mom stopped to kiss Hopie and to brush away her tears, but she didn't ask why she was crying.

"Try to get some sleep tonight, Liza," Mom told me. "And thanks for helping out." She kissed me on the forehead and went on downstairs.

"Good night, Mom," I said. "Tell Dad good night, too. And tell him...that I love him."

Chapter Three

The next afternoon, at exactly the same time as the day before, I turned onto Bayberry and walked by all those familiar houses. They were houses I had seen every single day of my life, but that day they looked subtly different. Bleak, somehow. Perhaps it was the gray day and the fine flakes of snow that were beginning to fall. More likely, it was my mood.

I crossed the street to our house, noticing that a light was on in the living room and that the paper had been taken in. I checked the mailbox. Empty. Someone was home. Carrie? Brent?... *Dad?*

I raced up the walk and burst through the front door. "Hello?" I called.

"Hi, sweetheart." Mom was sitting in the living room reading *The Story About Ping* to Hopie.

"Mom!" I cried. "You're home! Why are you home? You picked Sissy up early."

Hope gazed at me solemnly.

"I left school at noon to go to the hospital and decided to come home early. I got Hope on the way."

"Oh," I said. I wasn't sure if that was good or bad.

"Listen," said Mom. "What time will Brent and Carrie be home? I can't keep everybody's schedules straight."

"They should both be home soon. Brent doesn't have any after-school activities today."

"Good," replied Mom. "I want to talk to all of you again."

I started to ask Mom a question, but she silenced me with her eyes and went back to *Ping*.

Hope, I noticed, was strangely quiet. She'd been quiet at breakfast, too.

I fixed myself a snack and waited.

Brent and Carrie arrived home within ten minutes, and Mom called them into the living room before they even had a chance to eat anything.

The four of us kids sat down rather stiffly and waited while Mom paced back and forth. At last she stopped.

"Well," she said, "Dr. Keene, the cardiologist, spent some more time with your father this morning. And he has the results of several of the tests they took yesterday." Mom pressed her hands together. She paused.

"And?" prompted Brent.

"And he thinks your father has something called cardiomyopathy. That's just a long word meaning that his heart isn't functioning well anymore.... The prognosis isn't very good."

"What's 'prognosis'?" asked Carrie.

"The...outcome," replied Mom. "The prediction for the course the disease will take, the way things will turn out."

"What do you mean?" I whispered.

"Dad's heart is growing weaker every day. It's already far weaker than a normal heart. That's why he feels so tired and gets so short of breath. His heart has to work twice as hard as usual in order for him to climb stairs, to walk, to do just about anything. And no heart can stand the strain that's being put on your father's heart."

"But what exactly are you saying?" I persisted. "Is Dad going to die?"

"We're all going to die," snapped Carrie.

"Jerk! You know what I mean."

"Liza, Carrie, that's enough. No fighting now. I mean it." Mom's voice rose, and then dropped to a whisper. "We need each other too much."

I lowered my eyes.

"To answer your question, Liza," Mom said, and now her voice was quavering slightly, "he probably won't live much longer. Dr. Keene said anywhere from six months to a year."

I glanced quickly at Hopie. She was leafing through the pages of *Ping*. Brent and Carrie remained silent, staring at Mom. I stared, too. I couldn't believe it. We'd just been given the worst news of our lives, and we weren't falling apart. The O'Haras are from pretty strong stock.

"So what I think we have to do," Mom went on, "is make these last months the best ever."

That was followed by the loudest silence you can imagine.

I'm sure we were all thinking the same thing: was Mom crazy? These were going to be terrible months. Our *father* was *dying.* And Mom thought we could be happy? But before any of us said a word, we realized what Mom really meant: that, of course, we had to make the last months as good as we could—for Dad's sake.

"I get it," said Carrie. "We'll do this for Dad."

"And for *us,*" Mom said. "So that later we can look back to this time and find *nice* memories."

Silence again.

"When's Dad coming home from the hospital?" Brent asked finally.

"In about a week," said Mom. "Dr. Keene isn't quite finished with the tests, and he wants to try your father on several medications that will help him out during the next few months."

I glanced at Hopie again. She was still looking through *Ping,* her thumb in her mouth. I wondered just how much of this she understood. She'd been right here with the rest of us and had heard everything Mom had said. And yet she'd barely moved except to turn the pages in the book. She hadn't even looked up when Carrie and I had snapped at each other. But Hopie is smart. I knew she probably understood plenty.

"Well," said Mom briskly. "You guys are off dinner duty tonight. I'm not going back to the hospital until the evening, so—for today—you're off the hook. I'm cooking."

"Okay," said Carrie uncertainly. She got slowly to her feet, looking numb. I knew she wanted to be by herself.

"All right," said Brent. "I'm going...out."

"Play school with me, Liza," begged Hopie. She tossed aside *The Story About Ping* and ran to me. "Please? You can be the teacher."

"Not now, Sissy," I said picking her up, "but how about if you play school with your dolls? Then *you* can be the teacher."

Hopie looked disappointed, but left anyway.

I looked at Brent shrugging into his down jacket and Hopie and Carrie going upstairs. I listened to the sounds of Mom in the kitchen, opening and closing the refrigerator door, pouring out dog kibbles for Fifi, opening something with the electric can opener.

I decided to go over to Denise's, so I stuck my head into the kitchen to tell Mom. And I saw something that made me freeze. My mother was sitting at the kitchen table sobbing, the box of kibbles beside her. Her face was in her hands and her shoulders were shaking.

I backed away. I couldn't go to her. What would I say? I just left quietly for Denise's, feeling shattered. I had never, ever seen my mother fall apart like that.

Denise Petersen and her family moved to Bayberry seven years ago, just before Denise and I entered kindergarten. We didn't become friends right away, though, not even after we wound up in the same kindergarten class. We had to work up to it, skirting warily around each other for weeks. Then one day I spilled poster paint while I was at one of the easles, and Randy Norton, whom Denise and I hated, called me a "stupid, clumsy cow." So Denise ran up to him and kicked him in the shins. Our friendship was sealed.

I stood at the Petersens' front door, waiting for someone to answer the bell, and thinking about Denise and how she always roots for the underdog. She has a heart of gold—and a fiery temper. Denise is a great person to have on your side, but she can be a rotten enemy.

Right now I was trying to decide whether to tell her about my father. I knew she would be sympathetic, but I wasn't sure I wanted to talk about it yet. Besides, Denise would be more than sympathetic—she'd be crushed. Denise loved Dad, partly because Dad was so terrific and partly because Denise's own father had died several years ago. After that, she had kind of counted on my father for certain things, things her mother and younger sister, Maggie, couldn't help her with, like fixing the chain on her bike and showing her how to build a cage for her guinea pigs.

I had just resolved not to say anything to Denise—yet—when she answered the door, her face cloudy, and greeted me with, "How come you didn't tell me your father was in the hospital?"

She held the door open and I went inside, unzipping my jacket.

"How did you find out?" I asked.

"Cathryn Lynn's mother was working at the hospital this morning and saw him there. She told Cathryn Lynn after school and Cathryn Lynn told me. What is it? Some kind of secret?"

"No," I said. "I just don't feel like talking about it. Besides, it's no big deal, just one of those embarrassing little things." I couldn't believe I'd just lied to Denise.

Denise giggled. We have this joke about hemorrhoids, and I'm sure she thought that was what was wrong with Dad. "Okay," she said. "I'm sorry I was mad. It's just that we don't usually keep things from each other."

That was the truth. I told Denise *everything*. She knew things my mother didn't know and Carrie didn't know. She knew what had *really* happened to the brand-new sweater I told Mom was stolen at school. She knew about the time Brent and I experimented with the stuff in Mom and Dad's liquor cabinet until I started throwing up. (Mom thought I had a virus.) And she knew that, more than anything else in the world, I wanted to have a boyfriend.

How could I not tell Denise about Dad? But I couldn't. Not yet.

"Hey," I said, to get her mind off the subject, "did you get that new eye stuff?"

"Oh, yeah!" cried Denise. "Blushing Plum. It's great. Come on upstairs."

In Denise's room, we tried on her new makeup. Then we talked about cute boys. I thought Marc Radlay was the cutest boy in the whole seventh grade.

"Do you want to get married someday?" Denise asked me a little later. She was lying on her stomach on the floor, leafing through the pages of *Mademoiselle*. I was sacked out on her bed, thinking.

"Of course," I answered. "Don't you?"

"I don't know...."

I looked at Denise. She is absolutely beautiful. She has soft, straight blond hair and big blue eyes with impossibly long dark lashes. She could have stepped right out of *Mademoiselle*. And she could have had tons of boyfriends if she'd wanted. But she was very cautious.

"You don't want to get married?" I asked. "Don't you want kids?"

"Oh, you can have kids without getting married. People do it all the time."

"Yeah...but come on. Really. Why don't you want to get married?"

Denise sighed. She rolled over on her back and stared up at the ceiling. "You know what Mom said the day after Dad died?"

"No," I said, propping myself up on my elbows, suddenly very curious. I rolled over and looked at her. "What did she say?"

"She said, and these are her exact words, this is a direct quote: 'I won't get remarried, baby. It hurts too much to lose someone. I couldn't go through this again.'

When she first said that, I was relieved because, you know, I'd heard all those stories about stepparents, and the last thing I wanted was a new father. But then I thought about it some more and I decided that if losing your husband really hurts *that* much, maybe it isn't worth it. I mean, maybe getting married isn't worth it."

"Denise," I ventured, "how did *you* feel when your father died?"

Denise thought for a while. "Well," she said at last, "you know how you feel when you fall down really hard or when you get punched in the stomach—like you've had the wind knocked out of you?"

I nodded, even though I've never been punched in the stomach.

"That's how I felt. Surprised. And shocked. But mostly very scared, like when you panic because you think you're not going to get your breath back. I guess that's because it was so sudden."

Denise's father had died of something called an aneurysm. He was only thirty-six years old.

"How long did you feel that way?"

"I don't know. I don't remember. A few weeks? It just sort of wore off gradually. But I felt sad for a long, long time. For months, I guess. Sometimes I still feel sad. See, the thing is, there are other people who love me—Mom and Maggie and Gramma and your family—but there's nobody who will ever love me the way Dad did, because he was my father. You can't... replace that, you know?"

Denise took her gaze away from the ceiling and turned to look at me. I was crying. I couldn't help it.

"Liza!" Denise sounded shocked. I didn't blame her. "What's wrong?"

"Dad's not in the hospital having hemorrhoids fixed," I sobbed. I'm sure Denise could barely understand me. I was crying so hard all the words were rushing together. "He has this heart thing." I tried to remember the name Mom had given it.

"He has what?" Denise got up and sat beside me on the bed. She took one of my hands in hers.

"This... *heart* thing. I can't remember.... But he's going to *die*, Denise. The doctor says he won't live more than a year."

Denise put her arms around me and began to cry, too. "I'm sorry," she kept saying. "I'm sorry." I knew she felt as though she were losing her father all over again.

We sat there and cried for at least five minutes. Then we sniffled and sighed for fifteen or twenty more. But when we finally stopped, I felt very relieved. I hoped Denise did, too.

"Don't tell the kids at school yet, okay?" I asked Denise.

"Okay. I won't say a word." Denise stared at my eyes. "You look terrible. You want to wear the Blushing Plum to school tomorrow?"

I grinned. Life would go on. Not the same as usual, but it would go on.

Chapter Four

During the next few days, two important things happened. First of all, Mr. Landi held the auditions for the pageant. I had been wrapped up in a cocoon of worry about Dad and had completely forgotten about the pageant, the auditions, everything. I was lucky to remember where I lived. So when English class began one afternoon with Mr. Landi handing out scripts for *A Christmas Carol,* I was startled, to say the least.

"Class," he said, "our part in the pageant will be a production of this updated version of Dickens's classic Christmas story. I would like each one of you to be in the play. There are plenty of nonspeaking parts for those of you who are...who have a touch of stage fright." He glanced at me. I had sort of a reputation at Neuport Middle School. "The auditions are very casual. In fact, I'm going to hold them today."

This news was greeted with groans from all the kids

who wanted time to prepare or who (like me) had planned to miss the auditions somehow.

But Mr. Landi was firm. He gave us fifteen minutes to read the script. Then he asked for a show of hands of those students who wanted speaking parts. He listened to them read. And that was it. I didn't have to do anything.

Imagine my surprise when I walked into school the next day, looked at the posting of the assigned roles Mr. Landi had tacked to the bulletin board, and found out I'd been cast as the Spirit of the Future. I just about died. That sounded like a huge role.

Mr. Landi pulled me aside when he saw how upset I was. "Don't worry, Liza," he told me. "It's not as bad as you think. It's a nonspeaking role. I needed someone tall for it. You seemed like the perfect choice."

"Perfect," I repeated. I was dumbstruck.

Me, the Spirit of the Future...

The second important thing happened the following day when Dad came home. Mom hadn't known exactly when the doctors would spring him, so it was a nice surprise to run into 25 Bayberry after school and find him sitting in the living room with Hope in his lap.

"Dad!" I cried. I dropped my books on the floor and ran to him, throwing my arms around him. He smelled of soap and after-shave. He'd probably just taken a shower.

"Daddy's *back*," Hopie exclaimed. She sounded

awed. I hoped she didn't think he'd already died and had come back to us.

"Liza, I *missed* you!" Dad said. "Boy, is it good to be home. No more hospital food!"

I stood back to look at Dad. He seemed, well, okay. His eyes were sparkling, but his face looked sort of gray, and I had a feeling he'd lost some weight.

"I missed you, too," I said. Suddenly I wished I were little enough to sit in his lap like Hopie and feel his arms gather me up protectively. I knew why Hopie liked to sit in laps so much. It was because she felt safe that way—all folded in and loved.

"Where's Mom?" I asked.

"Picking up some work at school. She'll be home in about an hour."

I nodded.

"Emmy," Dad said to Hope, "could you please go get me a glass of water?"

"Sure," said Hope, eager to please. She scrambled out of his lap and ran into the kitchen.

"Dad," I began, when Hope was out of earshot. I sat on the floor at his feet. "I think Hope thinks...that you..."

"I know," he answered. "Your mother and I realized that when we picked her up at the HECC this afternoon. We'll just have to be very frank with her during the next months."

Dad was being frank, all right. I hadn't known how he would feel about talking about what was going on. But he was just *talking* about it, as if he were talking about what he was going to wear tomorrow. How could he do that?... And why should he have to do that?

I could feel tears welling up in my eyes. "Dad," I whispered.

Dad reached down and stroked my hair. But all he said was, "Not now, sweetheart, okay?"

I swallowed the lump in my throat just as Hopie came back, carrying the glass of water as if it might jump out of her hands at any moment, and Brent burst through the front door.

I moved to an armchair and leaned back into it, holding Charlie, who had appeared and jumped into my lap. Then I watched everybody as if they were actors in a play and I were a member of the audience.

I watched Dad greet Brent. Then I watched Dad swallow four huge pills. I watched Hopie take the glass back to the kitchen, proud to be able to help. And I watched Carrie arrive home and fling herself at Dad. All the while Charlie slept soundly, his head resting against my stomach.

When Mom got home later, Dad and us kids were still sitting around the living room.

"What a nice scene!" Mom exclaimed, putting her briefcase down. Mom likes nice scenes.

"Hi, Mom," Carrie and I said.

"Hi, Mommy," Hope said.

"What's for dinner?" Brent asked.

"I'm glad you asked," replied Mom, "although you do realize that you should be cooking tonight, don't you?"

"Yeah," said Brent guiltily.

"Well," said Mom, "I thought we could either go out to celebrate"—I saw her glance at Dad, and I saw Dad shake his head ever so slightly—"or," Mom went on without missing a beat, "we could send out for a pizza or for Chinese food."

At the mention of Chinese food, Hopie threw herself out of Dad's lap and began leaping around the living room, more animated than I'd seen her since the night we found out Dad had gone into the hospital.

"Chinese, Chinese, Chinese, please, please, please, please, *please!* Can we get egg ropes and chicken flied rice and chopped phooey, *please?*" Hope jumped up and down.

Everyone began laughing and trying not to show it.

"I guess we'll send out for Chinese food," Dad said. He was smiling, but he looked kind of relieved at the same time. I realized he hadn't moved out of the chair since I'd come home. And twice he had leaned his head back and closed his eyes for a few seconds. Why didn't he have more energy? He'd just had a whole week of bedrest. "Emmy, baby, go get the menu, okay?" he asked Hope.

Hope galloped into the kitchen and returned with the menu from Chef Ho's Hunan House. We put in a huge order. The food arrived an hour later, and we sat down to a real family meal, the six of us together again.

"Mmm. Yum-*yum*," said Hope. "An egg rope. My favorite."

"It's called an egg *roll*," Carrie corrected her.

"That's what I said."

Carrie giggled.

When everyone had been served, Dad said, "So tell me what you guys have been up to. I feel as if I've been away for a year instead of a week." He reached for his fork.

We all began talking at once. Brent told him about this wreck of a car he and Jeff Wilmont were supposedly fixing up. Carrie told him about a math test she'd gotten a 97 on, and Hopie told him about her school, of course.

"It's almost Christmas," she exclaimed, crunching on a large water chestnut. (There were still five weeks until Christmas.) "We're going to make macaroni chains for our trees. And we're going to make snowflakes. And a Santa Claus. And presents. And we're going to go to church to see the navy."

"The *what?*" gulped Carrie.

"The Nativity?" suggested Dad.

"Yeah. That."

"And you, Liza?" asked Dad.

Hopie had reminded me of our winter pageant. I decided to break the news to my family. "You won't believe this," I began, "but there's going to be this winter pageant at school. Our whole class is going to be in it."

"Your whole class?" ventured Mom. "You, too?"

Everyone was looking at me. They were remembering when I fainted before I gave my book report. They were remembering how I quit piano lessons because I couldn't handle the recitals. They were re-membering how I had to leave my own tenth birthday party because there were too many people watching me open presents.

I cleared my throat. "Yeah. Me, too."

Dad finally asked the question all the others wanted to ask. "What are you going to be ... or do?"

I sighed. "Our class is putting on an updated version of *A Christmas Carol*. I'm the Spirit of the Future. They needed someone tall."

"Isn't that sort of a ... major role?" Brent asked care-fully.

"Yeah. It is. But the Spirit of the Future doesn't speak. I don't have any lines."

"Well, that's something," said Carrie.

"I want to ask a huge favor of you right now," I said to my family. "I don't want any of you to come to the pageant. I mean it. I'm going to be horrible and I don't want you to see me. You'll make it worse." I looked at Dad. I can usually count on him to understand things like this.

"Well, honey," he said, "we'd like to see you in the pageant, of course, but if you don't want us to come, we won't. Why don't you wait until the pageant, though, and make up your mind then, okay?"

"Okay. I won't want you to come, but I'll wait."

"Fair enough." Dad smiled at me.

Mom changed the subject. "Thanksgiving is just a week off," she said.

Thanksgiving. I'd almost forgotten about it.

We started talking about what we wanted to do. Before we'd decided on anything, we'd finished dinner and leaned back in our chairs. Hope was rubbing her eyes.

"I think it's time for this little bunny to be in bed," said Dad.

"Will you take me, Daddy?" Hope asked.

"Honey, Daddy's too—" Mom started to say, but Dad was already on his feet.

"Sure, come on, Emmy."

While Dad put Hope to bed, Mom and Brent and Carrie and I cleared the table.

"Family meeting in twenty minutes," Mom informed us.

"Without Tink?" I asked.

"Just this once," said Mom.

Twenty minutes later we were in the living room. Dad sat between Carrie and me on the couch, his arms around us.

Charlie trotted into the room. *Mrow?* he asked, and bounded lightly into my lap. I stroked him as Mom began talking.

"You all know what the doctors have been saying."

We nodded. I glanced sideways at Dad. He was looking at Mom.

"You know that there's really not much we can do. Apparently, a heart transplant isn't what Dad needs—"

"What about an artificial heart?" Brent interrupted. Mom sighed.

"We don't want that," said Dad. "It's not worth it for the few extra weeks of life it might bring."

"So you mean we just sit around and wait for you to die?" Brent said explosively.

"Brent!" I exclaimed.

"It's all right, Liza," Dad said. "Brent, you have every right to feel angry. I feel angry, too, and cheated. I won't be able to see what you kids do with your lives. I won't even be able to see Hope grow up. I—" Dad's voice sounded choked. He took his arm from around me and dabbed at his eyes with a shaking hand.

Then I began to cry, too. So did Carrie. And Mom. And Brent. For a few minutes, the five of us sat there silently, brushing at tears and swallowing hard. Nobody spoke. After a couple of minutes, Dad took a handkerchief out of his pocket and blew his nose. Then he reached for Carrie's hand and mine.

"Well," he said, his voice returning to normal, "we have a year, maybe. And Christmas is coming soon. So we've got one terrific Christmas left together. Let's concentrate on that. There's a lot to do. We've got gifts to buy and decorations to make and food to bake."

I began to smile. Dad is like a little kid about Christmas. He plays carols on the stereo in July because he can't wait until December. He likes Christmas secrets. He buys gifts for almost everybody in the world. He's always made Christmas a magic time of year for our family.

We began planning things. Mom said we were going to buy Hopie a two-wheel bicycle. Dad said he wanted to buy chestnuts so we could roast them in the fireplace. Brent asked casually if he could a have a car, and Dad told him he was living in Fantasyland. We laughed.

A little while later, Dad and I were alone in the living room. He was still holding my hand.

"Dad?" I said. "You don't have to answer this, but I was just wondering. Do you think you'll miss things after you're ... gone?"

"Well, I don't know, Liza. I suppose so."

"What do you think you'll miss the most?"

Dad thought. Then he gave a little laugh. "I'd like to say I'm going to miss Peanut M&M's or football, or that I'm *not* going to miss poison ivy, or something like that, but it wouldn't be true. I'm just going to miss my family. You kids and your mom. In a way, you know, we're lucky," said Dad.

"Lucky? Us?" I asked.

"Only in that we have time to prepare for the death. We'll have a chance to say everything to each other during the next few months that we want or need to say.

"I think the hardest kind of death," continued Dad, "is a sudden one. Because of all the things left unsaid. There can be a lot of guilt that way." He paused. "Things left unsaid," he repeated slowly.

"Let's try to say everything," I suggested.

"Deal," agreed Dad.

I laid my head on Dad's shoulder. In my lap, Charlie stirred, rearranged himself, and went back to sleep.

Dad and I sat together until he said he had to take some pills.

Chapter Five

Two days later, I was sitting on the front porch with
Charlie. Mom and Dad were inside, Brent was out
back somewhere, and Carrie was walking Hope down
the street to the Whites' house to play with Susie and
Mandy.

"Charlie-man," I said, "if cats could make wishes,
what would you wish for?"

Charlie looked at me as if he were trying to understand. He was perched on the top porch step, and I
was a few steps down, leaning against a railing. So he
was about at eye level. We had a little staring contest.
Charlie won.

"I'll tell you what I'd wish for," I said. "I'd wish for
Dad to get well. I guess that's a pretty obvious wish,
isn't it?"

Charlie ambled down the stairs and stepped delicately into my lap. Then he pushed his face against mine, giving me a cat kiss.

"Well, it's what I'd wish for anyway. And if you could, I bet you'd wish to meet a nice girl cat. Nicer than Mouse," I added as she came padding silently around a corner of the house and sat down a little distance away from us, "and have a litter of kittens together. You'd be a good daddy."

Charlie gave me another kiss. Then he turned his head toward the street. I turned my head, too, to see what had attracted his attention. Sometimes he would go after dogs. But the road was empty. The whole neighborhood was quiet.

"What is it, Charlie?" I asked. "There's nothing over there."

Charlie leaped off my lap, though, and bounded toward the street. I watched him go, his ginger tail held high. And just as he reached the sidewalk, I saw a car coming.

"Charlie! No!" I cried, jumping up. What was he doing by the street, anyway? He never went near it. He usually stayed in back of the house.

Charlie didn't stop. I don't think he ever saw the car.

I watched him run under the wheels in a yellow blur. Then I watched the driver, a young man, try to swerve around him, tires squealing, then speed up and zoom away when he realized what had happened.

"Charlie! Charlie!" I started screaming and couldn't stop. I raced halfway to him, then paused, afraid to go near him. He was just a very still, crumpled heap by the side of the road.

His head was lying in a pool of blood. I could see that much from where I stood.

From far away I heard voices. "Liza? Liza!" the voices called. It was Mom and Dad. Mom ran out the front door and Dad followed more slowly. Then Brent came around from behind the house. Across the street, the Washburns' garage door opened.

Suddenly people were everywhere. Mr. and Mrs. Washburn dashed to the roadside and saw Charlie, and Mrs. Washburn dashed back to their garage, then returned with some flares, which she set up in the road around Charlie's body. Brent stood by me with his arm across my shoulders. Dad knelt to examine Charlie, and Mom ran into the house to call the vet. Mr. Washburn took his sweater off and laid it over Charlie.

I saw all this very clearly and can remember every detail.

A few minutes later, Mom came back. She was carrying a small board. "We're supposed to slide Charlie on this and get him to the Pet Emergency Center as fast as we can," she said briskly.

"Nancy," my father said quietly, "I don't think there's really any p—"

"Of course there is. Brent, will you help me?"

Brent hurried to Mom and helped her get Charlie on the board. All I kept thinking was that Mr. Washburn's sweater was soaked with blood and we'd have to buy him a new one.

Fifi appeared and stood next to me, watching things worriedly and poking her wet nose into my hands.

Just as Mom and Brent pulled out of the driveway and Mrs. Washburn began taking the flares down, I saw Carrie and Denise across the street. I was glad Hope was at the Whites'. She didn't need to see this.

Denise ran across the street to me, but I didn't feel like talking to anybody. "I'm going to my room," I said. "I want to be alone." Charlie was dead. I knew that. The Pet Emergency Center couldn't do anything except ask Mom how she wanted to dispose of his body.

Denise nodded. "Okay," she said.

I started across the lawn to the house and the haven of my bedroom.

"Liza?" Dad called.

I turned but saw Denise talking to him. She must have told him what I'd said. He didn't call me again.

I reached the porch steps. Mouse was sitting contentedly on the top one, in the same spot where Charlie had been not long ago. Suddenly I hated her. I wanted to hurt her for being alive when Charlie was dead. So I did something terrible. I purposely stepped on her tail—hard—as I went past her.

Mouse shrieked with pain and surprise. She tore off the porch and into the bushes to nurse her tail. I ignored her and went to my room.

An hour later there was a knock on my door.

"What?" I said.

I'd been sitting on my bed all that time. Not crying, just sitting and staring and thinking. Once I'd gotten up to look out the window. I could see the bloodstain in the street.

Mom and Dad came in, followed by Denise.

"Honey," said Mom, "a doctor at the Center looked at Charlie right away, but he said there was nothing to be done. Charlie must have been killed instantly."

"I know," I said.

"They cleaned him up, though," said Dad, "and Mom and Brent brought him home. We thought it would be nice to bury him out back next to Spanky."

Spanky was the first cat we'd had. She'd died of old age when she was fourteen.

"Okay," I said. "But not right now."

"And," added Mom, "the vet said if we ever want to get another cat, the Center often has litters of orphaned kittens. They'd be glad to give us one. They always need people to give strays good homes."

"Mom," I said stiffly, "Dad, Denise—I do not want another cat. Do you understand?" I couldn't say anymore. I didn't want to start crying yet. I took two deep breaths while everyone began talking at once.

"Baby," began Dad.

"Honey," said Mom.

"Liza," Denise said.

But I cut them all off. "Would you please just get out of here? Please—leave—me—alone."

And they did, but the door hadn't been closed for

more than a minute when Hope let herself in.

"I'm sorry about Charlie," she said, crawling up beside me on the bed.

I sighed.

"Is he really dead?"

"Yes, Hopie. He's really dead."

"Mommy said that means we won't see him anymore."

"That's right. After we bury him, we won't see him anymore."

"Why do we bury him?"

"Could you please go ask Mom, Tink?" I said. "I don't want to talk about it."

"Are you sad?" asked Hopie.

"Yes. I'm sad."

"Well, don't worry. I know a secret."

"What?" I asked. I was losing my patience.

"He *will* be back," whispered Hope, leaning toward me conspiratorially. "Not right away. But later. He'll come back. Maybe in some days or some weeks." She nodded her head wisely, as if confirming this information.

"Look, Sissy," I said. "Will you do me a big favor? Will you go downstairs right now and talk about this with Mom and Dad? Tell them just what you told me."

"Why?" asked Hopie.

"Because I said."

"But it's a secret."

"They'll keep the secret. Okay?"

"All right."

Hopie left reluctantly.

Later that afternoon, we held a funeral for Charlie. Our whole family was there, plus Denise. The Pet Emergency Center had sent Charlie home in a plastic bag. We put the bag in a box.

Then Brent dug a hole in the ground under an ash tree next to an uneven piece of slate that said in faded white letters:

SPANKY
A Sweet Cat

We stood in a huddle in the warm sunshine and watched Brent place the box in the hole and start burying it with shovelfuls of dirt.

"Daddy," whimpered Hopie. "If Brent covers him up, he won't be able to get out."

"He *can't* get out, Emmy," Dad said firmly. "He's dead. That means he *won't come back*. Do you understand?"

Hope didn't answer. She just let her tears fall silently.

Brent finished burying Charlie.

Then I got the new piece of slate on which I'd carefully printed:

CHARLIE

That was all that was going on his gravemarker. I

didn't think anything else needed to be said. Carrie and Denise helped me push the marker into the frozen ground and prop it up with rocks.

Then I stood, brushing the dirt off my hands, and turned to my family. They were standing solemnly, facing the new grave. Suddenly nobody had anything to say. We just looked at each other. I knew we were all thinking the same thing. The next funeral would probably be Dad's.

Dad turned abruptly and started walking toward the house, Fifi at his side. We let him go.

Everybody managed to find something to do outdoors. We knew Dad needed to be alone. Denise and I walked back to the edge of our property and sat down in two ancient tire swings that hung from the branches of a gigantic old maple.

"I can't cry," I said to Denise. "All this week I cried about Dad, and now Charlie's *really* dead and I can't cry."

"I know," said Denise.

"You do?" I asked.

"Mm-hmm. When my dad died I couldn't cry at first either. I was too numb. Also, I was afraid to cry. It was like..." She paused, thinking. "It was like, the thing I had to cry over was *so* awful, I was afraid if I started, I'd never be able to stop. So I put it off for weeks. I kept telling myself I was strong and that only babies cried. I told myself I didn't need to cry. Then when I did, when I couldn't keep it inside any longer, it was pretty awful. That was the time when I wouldn't speak to you. And I stayed out of school for a whole week, remember?"

I nodded.

"Mom said I should have let myself cry earlier. She said even though it seemed awful then, it would have been easier. Maggie was so little, she cried right away and got over it, just as if she'd been stung by a bee or something. It wasn't so bad for her."

The sunny day was beginning to disappear as heavy clouds rolled in. I shivered. "It's cold," I said. "Let's go inside."

Denise shook her head. "I better go home. I've got to practice for my piano lesson. But come over tomorrow, okay?"

"Okay."

As we walked back toward my house, we came across Hopie, sitting behind the tool shed. Mouse was cradled in her arms. Her back was to us and she didn't see us, but I could hear her.

"I won't let them do that to you," she said. "No boxes, Mousie, I promise."

I glanced at Denise. "I better talk to her," I whispered. "See you tomorrow."

Denise left and I sat down on the ground next to Hope. "Do you know what 'dead' means?" I asked her.

Hope looked as if I'd said something dirty to her.

I went on before she could answer. "It means you're not alive anymore. It means you can't move or think or feel. It's like being asleep, except you can't dream.

You can't even *breathe*. There's nothing left of you except your body. Do you understand?"

Hope relaxed a little. "I guess..."

"Remember that bug you stepped on yesterday?"

"The one I squished?"

"Yeah. Do you think that bug can move around now? Do you think it can fly or crawl or sting people?"

"No," said Hope. "That was why I squished it."

"Well, now it's dead," I said. "Only, a living thing doesn't have to be squished to die. Animals and people can die in different ways. Today Charlie was hurt so badly that he died."

"Then he really isn't coming back?" Hope asked. "He's not trying to get out of the box?"

"He can't."

"Oh," she said. "Dead is dead."

"That's right."

I took her hand. "Let's go inside now."

So we did. And when we got there, we found the last thing I'd have expected. Dad was in the living room surrounded by cardboard cartons. Our Christmas decorations. He looked as happy as a clam.

"Girls! Oh, good. I know it's not even Thanksgiving yet, but around here, Christmas starts today!"

"But Dad, if we decorate now, we won't have any decorating to do later."

"Oh, come on, just a *little*?"

I grinned. Dad really couldn't wait any longer!

"Go find your mother and Brent and Carrie," he said. "Let's start!"

"Yay!" shouted Hopie.

So Christmas at 25 Bayberry began five days before Thanksgiving that year. And that night, I let myself cry about Charlie.

Chapter Six

Thanksgiving came and went. In our family, it has always been a happy affair, sometimes with guests, sometimes not; but it has always seemed overshadowed by the Christmas that is drawing near.

That year it seemed particularly overshadowed. Dad's desire for one last perfect Christmas had worked its way into each one of us. Christmas was all we could think of.

We began our Christmas shopping the day after Thanksgiving, and everyone had big ideas. Mine were so big I had to ask Mom if I could dip into my savings account so I'd have enough money to buy everything. I was only slightly surprised when she said yes without even hesitating. No doubt about it, we were pulling out all the stops that Christmas.

Hopie had big ideas too, but they all involved herself. (She hadn't quite gotten the hang of *giving* gifts.)

She wrote an early letter to Santa asking for bunk beds, a bicycle, a dollhouse, a new swing set, a horse, a playhouse, and a few other things. Dad blanched slightly as she dictated the letter to him.

Even knowing what was going to happen to Dad, I think I could have forgotten a little and really enjoyed our frantic Christmas preparations, except for one thing. Dad was getting worse.

He had told the company he worked for about his health and the prognosis, and Dad's boss had said that his job and his office would be there for him as long as he liked. But Dad usually managed to go to New York only twice a week, and then sometimes only for a half a day. I began to worry about money, but Dad said he was still being paid his full salary.

One night I woke up with a start. I squinted at the digital alarm clock by my bed. It read 3:15. What had woken me up? I didn't need to go to the bathroom, and there was no more Charlie needing to be let in or out.

Then I heard a creak in the hallway, and another creak. Sometimes Carrie walked in her sleep. I got up to see if she needed any help, but it wasn't Carrie I found in the dark hall; it was Dad.

He was pacing back and forth, breathing fast and noisily.

"Dad!" I cried. "What's the matter?"

Pant, pant. "Nothing *(pant)* to worry about." *Pant, pant.* "Just have to *(pant)* catch my breath."

"Why? What were you doing?"

"Just sleeping *(pant)*. It's *(pant)* hard to catch my breath *(pant)* at night sometimes."

I think Dad was trying to reassure me, but he looked scared and sort of gray all over. I took his hand. "Why don't you go back to bed? Maybe you'll feel better lying down." I was hoping we would "accidentally" wake Mom as Dad got in bed. She'd know what to do.

But Dad shook his head. "Just need to walk around *(pant)* a little until I can breathe better *(pant)*. It's already getting easier."

"Well, let's go downstairs," I suggested.

"All right."

I flicked on the light that lit the stairway and led Dad down to the living room. Then I got an idea. "How about some hot chocolate?" I suggested.

"Well...okay." Dad began to smile.

He sat in the kitchen while I heated up a pan of milk.

I listened to him breathing. He did sound better. Noisy and a bit ragged, but definitely better.

When the hot chocolate was ready, we sat at the table sipping it slowly. I was glad Dad was drinking it. Maybe he would put on a pound or two.

"How's the play coming?" he asked.

"Oh, what a *joke*. Dad, it's supposed to be an *up*-dated version of *A Christmas Carol*, so there are all these stupid things in the script."

"Such as?"

"Such as Scrooge is an insurance salesman, and Bob Cratchit's kids earn money doing things like delivering papers and baby-sitting. And for Christmas dinner, Mrs. Cratchit makes a *meat loaf*. And for dessert, she makes a *Jello-O mold*."

Dad laughed. His breathing sounded almost normal. "Oh, Liza."

"What?"

"You've got a wonderful sense of how things should be. Don't ever lose that, even if sometimes it seems too idealistic for this harsh world of ours. You're the quiet one in this family. You're sandwiched between Brent's mouth and your two chatterbox sisters. I see you sitting back and taking things in, just listening and watching and storing up what's going on around you. I know you're forming opinions, maybe even judging us sometimes, and that's okay. I think you'll put your mind to good use someday. In fact, you're already putting it to good use, but not everyone knows it because you're so quiet."

"I might write," I said slowly.

"Be a writer?" Dad asked. "Mom and I would be very proud of you."

"No. Just write. I keep a diary, but I don't write in it very often. Mostly I write in my head. I remember things...." I wasn't sure how to explain this. I'd never tried before.

"Well, I imagine you'll get all those 'things' sorted out one day and put them down on paper."

I nodded.

We'd finished our hot chocolate. I carried the empty mugs to the sink and rinsed them out.

"Do you think you can sleep now?" I asked Dad.

"I think so."

Chapter Seven

The day we had our first full dress rehearsal for the pageant was the day I definitely made up my mind that I didn't want anyone to go to it.

"Believe me, you won't be missing a thing," I announced at dinner.

"But I want to see you be a ghost," said Hopie, her lower lip trembling.

"I'll bring my costume home and give you a special, private performance. How's that, Sissy?"

"Okay," said Hope.

"Really," I continued, glancing back and forth from Mom to Dad, "I don't want anyone to come. I'm not just saying that. I mean it."

"Then we won't come," said Dad.

"Are you sure you don't want just one person there for moral support?" Mom asked.

"Yeah," said Carrie. "What if you faint?"

"I won't faint." But it occurred to me that fainting into Marc Radlay's arms might be sort of interesting. Marc, who I still thought was the cutest boy in our grade, was Scrooge, so I played my entire scene with him. I imagined myself on the stage, beginning to sway ever so slightly. Marc would notice and stop speaking in the middle of one of his monologues.

"Liza?" he would whisper, trying not to attract too much attention.

And right then and there I'd keel over, and Marc would catch me and lay me gently on the stage. The audience would murmur and gasp as Marc would bend over to touch his lips to my forehead....

I was replaying that daydream for the tenth or eleventh time in bed that night when I heard voices downstairs. I'd thought everyone was asleep.

I threw back the covers, tiptoed across my bedroom, opened the door a crack, and stood listening for a few seconds. I didn't intend to eavesdrop; I just wanted to make sure everything was all right.

Mom's and Dad's voices floated up to me from the living room.

"...respect a person's wishes...," I heard Dad say softly.

And I froze. What was going on? Were they talking about his *funeral*? Had something happened that I didn't know about?

I crept further down the hall, stopping abruptly when a floorboard creaked.

"I know she means it," Dad said, and I let out a sigh

of relief. They weren't talking about Dad's last wishes after all.

"Maybe if you explained to her," Mom suggested gently.

"No," said Dad. "I don't want to put any extra pressure on the kids. These months are tough enough on them as it is."

Mom murmured something I couldn't make out.

"It's just that I want to be a part of everything while I can," Dad went on. "I don't want to miss out on a thing. Who knows? Liza could grow up to be a great actress."

"Not with her stage fright," Mom said. I could tell she was smiling.

I didn't want to hear Dad's response. I'd heard plenty. I went back to my room and pulled up the window shade. Then I knelt on the bed and looked out on our moonlit street. It had snowed again, so the world was frosty white.

At that moment, I wished more than anything that Charlie were with me. He'd always liked the nighttime and my windowsill, and he'd been good company when someone was feeling sad.

But there was no Charlie.

I sat by the window anyway.

So Dad wanted to come to the pageant. He wanted to see me in a school performance. He wanted to share that piece of my life with me. I could understand that.

But now what was I supposed to do? I wasn't supposed to know that he wanted to come. I couldn't change my mind and invite the family, since I'd told them several times how bad the play was. And besides, I really didn't want everyone there. Maybe I could think of a reason to invite just Dad.

I flopped down on my bed and decided to worry about it in the morning.

And I did. Worry, I mean. But it didn't get me anywhere, except in trouble. I worried about it before school and I worried about it during school. I worried so much that I practically ruined the rehearsal that afternoon.

I was sitting in the auditorium completely lost in thought, and didn't notice when Act III wound up, which was my cue to get ready for the scene I played with Marc. I didn't notice anything until I realized that the auditorium was dead silent. Marc was on stage alone—waiting for me. I looked around. The whole class was staring at me. I flushed deeply, my face growing hot.

"Liza?" said Mr. Landi. "Would you care to join Marc on the stage, or do you just want to test the seats in the auditorium all afternoon?"

I hate sarcasm. I really hate it.

I wondered what would have happened if I'd said I preferred to test the seats, but I didn't try it.

"Sorry!" I cried. I grabbed my costume and ran behind the stage. Then I joined Marc in Act IV. And I was a disaster. I tripped over my Spirit robe—twice—

and stepped on Marc's foot. I could hear the kids snickering backstage.

As soon as the rehearsal was over, I fled from school and burst into tears on the way home. There I was, crying right out in the open, when I heard Denise calling me.

"Liza!" she shouted. "Wait up!" She ran across the street, juggling her school books and her piano music. "I can't believe it," she said breathlessly. "Our class isn't supposed to be in the pageant, so I thought I'd gotten out of it, but guess who has to play the piano during—" She stopped when she got a good look at my face. "Hey, what's wrong? Is it...your dad?"

I shook my head, wiping away my tears. "No," I replied. I told her what had happened at rehearsal.

"Oh," she said. "Well, look, so you ruined one scene. You think the play is dumb anyway."

"I know, but everyone laughed at me. And I stepped on Marc's foot. On *Marc's* foot. Why couldn't I have stepped on someone else? I mean, if I had to step on somebody."

Denise smiled. "He's probably already forgotten about it."

"He's probably already bruised and limping. How am I ever going to get through the play?"

"Well, now I'll be there playing the piano. I'll give you moral support. And Margie Mason will be backstage with you. You're pretty good friends, and she's in the same boat. She can give you moral support, too."

"Moral support!" I exclaimed. "Hey, that's it! Oh, thanks, Denise! I love you!"

"What?" Denise was still smiling, but she looked totally confused.

"I have to go," I told her. "I have to tell Dad something. I'll call you later. 'Bye!"

I ran the rest of the way home.

Dad was in the living room. Obviously, he'd been wrapping Christmas presents. Tissue paper, ribbon, gold trim, paper decorations, gift tags, scissors, and bottles of glue were strewn everywhere. But Dad was stretched out on the couch with an afghan over him, breathing noisily.

He opened his eyes when I came in. "Hi, sweetheart," he said.

"Hi. Are you okay?" I asked.

"Just tired. I thought I'd rest up before dinner."

He was tired from wrapping presents?

I sighed.

Then I sat down next to him on the edge of the couch.

"How was school?" he asked.

"School was all right. The rehearsal stank."

"What happened?"

"It just stank, that's all. But I was thinking. Remember what Mom said last night about someone being at the pageant to give me moral support?"

Dad nodded.

"Well, I think that's a good idea. I think I might need moral support. But I still don't want everyone to see

the play. It'll be too embarrassing. What I was wondering, though, was if *one* person could come. I mean,
could *you* come? If you're not too tired?"

"Do you really want me to?"

"Yes. If you think Mom won't be hurt that I didn't
ask her."

"I think she'll understand."

"Okay. Then will you come?"

"Of course."

"Thanks, Dad."

The evening of the pageant was cold and still, the
air heavy with the promise of snow. Mom dropped Dad
and me off at school about a half an hour before show-
time (Dad wasn't allowed to drive anymore), and we
hustled inside, shivering. I found Dad a seat near the
front where I'd be sure to see him from the stage. Then
I ran down the hall to my classroom. *A Christmas
Carol* was the last performance of the evening, so we
were going to have to wait awhile before we could go
backstage. We busied ourselves with our costumes and
lines.

Margie Mason found me and examined me critically
as I put the finishing touches on my costume and
makeup. "You look really weird," she said at last.

"Thanks a lot!"

"No, I mean good weird, like the Spirit of the Future
should look."

"Really?"

Margie nodded.

I had to admit that I was wearing one of the better costumes. Outside of my billowy, hooded robe, nothing showed except my face and hands, and I had painted them green with greasepaint. My hair was slicked back so that I looked bald underneath the hood, and my fingernails were painted with fluorescent polish so they would glow faintly on the darkened stage.

"Thank goodness I don't have any lines," I said. "Do you need any help with yours?"

Margie shook her head. "I'm afraid to study them anymore. It'll be bad luck."

So we sat back and began the long wait until the handbell choir was on. That would be our cue to get ready backstage.

During the intermission, Denise stuck her head in the room. "How are you doing?" she asked.

"Okay. I have awful butterflies, but I can't wait to get this *over* with. How are you doing?"

"Not bad. I don't think I've made any mistakes that anyone noticed, but I had a terrible time accompanying the sixth-grade carol choir. They were completely off—off-key, off-beat, off-everything, and they didn't even notice."

"Make some mistakes while you're playing the background music for my scene," I suggested. "That'll take the attention away from Marc and me."

Denise giggled. "I'll see what I can do," she said, but we both knew she would never make mistakes on purpose.

Exactly thirty-seven minutes later I was waiting

backstage with most of the rest of my class. For once, everyone was silent. The play was on.

We could hear Marc reciting one of his monologues on the other side of the curtain. It was almost the end of Act III. In just a few minutes, I'd be out there on stage.

Margie must have been thinking the same thing since she came on later in my scene. She glanced at me nervously and I tried to smile at her, but it came out lopsided. I wanted to squeeze her hand, except that I would have turned it green.

"Break a leg," said Margie.

"You too."

The next thing I knew, I was onstage. The set was slowly brightening from almost pitch black to very dim. As I slowly crossed the stage to Marc, a hush settled over the audience. Whispers faded away and papers stopped rustling. I reached Marc, put my hand on his shoulder—and for one horrifying second, thought I really was going to faint, just like in the daydream.

Dad. Where was he? I glanced sideways at the audience. My knees were shaking, my hands were shaking. There were an awful lot of people in that audience.

Marc eyed me suspiciously as he began speaking. "Spirit of the Future!" he cried, and at that moment I found Dad. He nodded to me and gave me the thumbs-up sign.

I relaxed, turned my attention back to the play, and found that I was able to forget about the audience.

A few minutes later my role in the scene was over. I glided behind the curtain and let out a sigh of relief that could have been heard in Idaho. I'm certain the audience heard it. But I didn't care. The play was over!

Later, Dad found me backstage taking off the grease-paint.

"Dad!" I exclaimed. "How was it?"

Dad took his hands from behind his back and handed me a red rose. "A rose for a star," he said. "You did just fine, honey."

I took the rose and stared at it. Then I put my arms around Dad's neck and began to cry.

Dad held me for a long time. "Christmas," he said, finally. "We still have Christmas."

Chapter Eight

Christmas.

It seemed to come too quickly and too slowly at the same time. We'd been preparing for it for so long, starting when Dad got out the decorations before Thanksgiving, and yet, probably because I never wanted that Christmas to be over, the season seemed to speed by. It went by especially quickly after the pageant, because then I felt as if I could really relax.

The next weekend, I decided to finish my Christmas shopping. Everyone was up early on Saturday, so we ate breakfast together, which doesn't happen too often on the weekends. Dad was looking pretty good. He was even eating without Mom badgering him. We were making our plans for the day.

Carrie, who had a cold, was going to stay home and wrap her presents. Brent was going to go out to Thomp-

son's Tree Farm to bring home the tree we'd picked
out a few weeks earlier. Thompson's was a good forty-
five minutes outside of Neuport.

"Brent," I said, "could you drop me off at the mall
on your way to Thompson's?"

"Sure," he said.

"Shopping?" asked Mom.

I nodded.

"Could you take Sissy with you?"

I don't like to shop with Hope, and Mom knows that.
But she probably wanted to finish buying Hope's gifts
that day. How could I say no, especially with Hope
sitting right there at the table? Luckily, I'd already
finished my own shopping for Hopie.

"Okay," I said.

"Oh, goody, goody, goody!" cried Hope.

I glanced at Mom.

"She wants to visit Santa and ride on the train to
Santa's Village," Mom said, somewhat apologetically.

"And go to Candyland!" Hope added ecstatically.

Our mall was well equipped.

"Oh, all right," I said. "Can we make a bargain, Sissy?
I take you to Santa and the train and Candyland, and
then you take me shopping. I have six presents to
buy—that's a lot—and I want to buy them all today.
After we finish, we can eat lunch at Burger King. Is
that a deal?"

"Yes," said Hope, nodding her head.

"Are you sure? Six presents?"

"Yes," Hope said again. "I have to buy some things, too."

"How much money do you have?"

Hope looked at Dad, uncertain.

"I think she has five dollars," answered Dad, reaching for his wallet.

"Is that enough?" asked Hope.

I didn't have the vaguest idea what she wanted to buy.

"Probably," I said anyway. I wanted to get going. "If you need more, I'll lend you some."

Dad winked at me, so I knew that was okay and that he'd pay me back.

Suddenly I had an inspiration. "Dad, why don't you come with us?" I asked. He could watch Hope while I bought the presents that were for him, and I could take her when Dad needed to rest.

"Oh, I don't know," he said slowly.

I could tell he wanted to go very badly. There's nothing like the sight of Hope riding that train to Santa's Village. Her whole face lights up, her body tensed with a pleasure that's almost overwhelming for her.

"Come on, Dad. We can even bring the camera. And you can rest sometimes. There's that lounge by the children's play area. Next to the jeans store, you know?"

"I know...."

Lately, Dad was nervous about leaving the house. He hardly ever went to the office. But he wanted to be part of this bit of Christmas.

"*Please?*" begged Hope.

"Well, why not?" said Dad.

Mom smiled tightly. She was glad Dad would be getting out, but she, too, was nervous about it.

There really wasn't any reason for her to be nervous, as it turned out. Dad came along and we had a great time. We had to do Santa and the train first because Hope was so excited by the time we reached the mall that she literally couldn't wait a second longer. She pulled us past the stores, their windows shining with tinsel and holly and red and green lights, straight to Santa's train. It was gaudy and glittery, perfect for kids, and carried its passengers through the center of the mall, which had been turned into a snowy fairyland, to Santa's house. At the Neuport Mall, Santa apparently lived in a candy and gingerbread house.

There was a line of kids at the train, of course, but it wasn't very long. Hope waited as patiently as she could, but she was wiggling all over and bouncing around, asking a million questions. "Will Santa Claus remember me from last year? Do you think I've been good enough? Where's Rudolph?"

Then the train returned to the platform from its most recent run to Santa's Village, and when its passengers got off, Hope and four other children climbed into the little cars. Dad and I walked beside the track, Dad snapping pictures of Hope as the train chugged slowly through the mall.

Dad took a whole roll of photos of Hope at the mall, and in the months after Christmas looked at them again and again. They meant something to him, but I wasn't sure what, and he didn't talk about it.

The rest of the day was fun. I did finish my shopping, and we did take Hope to Candyland and to eat at Burger King, but nothing compared to her visit to Santa.

Two days before Christmas it snowed again. Hard. We woke up to a world of white. The ground was covered, the trees were covered, and still the snow was falling. It swirled and blew, looking just like a postcard of someone's idea of the perfect Christmas snow.

We were ready for Christmas. The house was decorated inside and out. Holly greens with gold lights were draped around the front door, and a huge wreath with wooden fruit and a red bow hung on the door. Carrie and Hope and I had decorated a little tree, "Santa's tree," in the yard. And candles were in every window.

Our shopping was finished, the presents were wrapped and carefully hidden, the baking was done. There was tremendous excitement in the air, and all sorts of secrets (Brent still thought he was getting a car), but mostly there was a feeling of moving toward something wonderful. At first I had thought of this as our last Christmas; now it had become, as Dad wanted, our best Christmas.

There was only one thing left to do—decorate the tree in the living room. We chose that snowy, snowbound day to do it. School was already closed, so we got an early start. Brent built a fire, I put carols on the stereo, and Carrie and Mom brought the boxes of decorations down from the attic. We see those decorations every year, but you'd never know it. We exclaim over them like long-lost friends.

"Oh, here are Grandmother's spun-glass birds!" cried Mom, opening a box.

"And here's the old wooden soldier," said Dad, opening another.

"Yuck," said Carrie, holding up a shapeless brown rope. "Here's my gross old macaroni chain from nursery school. Why do you still have it?"

"I don't think it's gross," said Hopie slowly, glancing at the shapeless brown chain she'd made the week before.

"They're both lovely," said Mom, hanging them on the bottom of the tree, sort of in back.

"Aghh!" shrieked Carrie. "Here's that angel I made from sea shells and pipe cleaners. And toilet paper! Her hair is made of toilet paper!"

Everyone laughed at that, even Hope, and we put it on the tree near the macaroni chains.

Dad surveyed our work from the couch, smiling, but not strong enough to stand up and help.

When the tree was finished, we turned off the lamps in the living room and turned on the tree lights. The tree glowed softly in the corner. It looked enchanted.

"Ooh," said Hopie. "Pretty. I love Christmas."

"Yeah," said Carrie, "me too. I—" She stopped abruptly, her gaze traveling to Dad, and I turned to look, too. He was leaning back against the couch with his hand clutching his chest. His face was a pasty white and he was gasping for breath.

My mother ran to him. "What is it?" she asked, trying to stay calm.

"Get my pills," Dad whispered.

Mom must have known which ones he meant, because there were at least four bottles of Dad's pills in the kitchen, but she came back with just one.

She slipped a pill under Dad's tongue, then sat next to him on the couch, clasping his hand and smoothing his hair from his forehead.

The rest of us just stared. We didn't even move until Brent said, "I'll call the ambulance."

My mother nodded.

"No." Dad struggled to sit up straighter.

But Brent called anyway, and the ambulance came a few minutes later and took Dad back to the Neuport Medical Center.

As the ambulance drove carefully down the slippery street, Brent and Carrie and I wordlessly turned off the tree lights, then the outside lights. We snuffed out the candles in the windows and let the fire in the fireplace die down.

"Why?" whimpered Hopie, watching us anxiously.

"It just doesn't feel right to let the house be so cheerful while Dad's in the hospital," I said.

"Are we still going to have Christmas?" asked Hope.

"Hope, shut *up*. I don't know."

Hope burst into tears and fled to her room.

* * *

But the next day, Dad came home.

"It wasn't serious," Mom told us before she left to pick him up. "They watched him overnight and said he's much better this morning. The doctors are just being extra cautious."

Dad was home in time for lunch. He looked, well, not exactly good, but a lot better than the day before.

We turned all the lights back on and built another fire. It was Christmas Eve! I couldn't help feeling excited. There were going to be an awful lot of surprises the next day.

Denise came over that afternoon and we exchanged gifts. She gave me a little makeup kit so I could start wearing eye shadow and stuff. And I gave her some funky bracelets.

"Oh!" she cried. "I can't wait to show these off at school!"

That night, our family spent the evening in the living room. We were enjoying ourselves, but there was something in us that didn't want us to be separated. We were clinging together while we went through our Christmas Eve ritual. After dinner, which is always clam chowder on Christmas Eve, we turned on the tree lights. Then we hung our stockings and Dad read *The Night Before Christmas* to us, with Hope curled up in his lap, looking dreamy, Mouse in *her* lap, and Fifi at Dad's feet. Then Mom read us the Christmas story from the Bible. After that, Hope put out milk and cookies for Santa Claus, and after *that*, it was her bedtime. The rest of us kids waited until she was asleep, then we ran around getting our gifts out of their hiding places and putting them under the tree. A little while later, Carrie and Brent and I went to our rooms, and Mom and Dad put their gifts out.

I fell asleep reading an Agatha Christie mystery and didn't wake up until I heard a little voice.

"Liza?" whispered the voice.

"Mmphh," I answered.

"Liza, it's Christmas!"

I struggled to open my eyes. Hope was standing at the foot of my bed, shivering in the chilly room.

"What time is it?" I asked her.

"I don't know. I can't tell time."

I rolled over and looked at my watch. Six o'clock. "You can wake everyone else up, I guess," I said. Six o'clock wasn't *too* early.

A little while later, another fire lit, the tree lights on, Mom and Dad allowed us kids to race downstairs. And what a sight the living room was! It looked like a department store. There was Hope's two-wheeler, a dollhouse, and a gigantic teddy bear. There was a ten-speed racing bike for Carrie, a tape deck for me, and even a new bed for Fifi, and a scratching post for Mouse.

"And look outside," Dad said to Brent. He parted the curtains and we all rushed to the window.

"What?" asked Brent.

"That," said Dad. He pointed to the street.

"That? That—that *car?"*

Dad nodded, grinning. "It's secondhand, but it's in good condition."

By that time we were all practically hysterical with excitement.

And there were more presents to go—all the wrapped ones under the tree. We spent hours opening them. Dad gave Mom a diamond bracelet. Mom gave Dad *The Collected Works of F. Scott Fitzgerald*.

Mom gave me a certificate that said I could get my ears pierced, and Carrie gave me a pair of wild earrings. Dad put on a funny flashing bow tie I had found for him. He turned it on whenever visitors arrived.

The day was magic, from beginning to end.

But nobody enjoyed it more than Dad.

BOOK II

Spring

Chapter One

In November, the doctors had said Dad would live for six months to a year. He lived for exactly six and a half months, until the beginning of June.

After Christmas, he was in and out of the hospital five times, for different reasons. But in the middle of May, he came home for good, his body spent and tired. He lived his last days in bed, his muscles wearing out, his legs often swollen, an oxygen tank always in the room. And then one Tuesday he simply slipped away.

We had known it would happen then, and Mom had kept us kids home from school. The evening before, while Dad slept, she had called us together. "It won't be much longer," she had said. "All his vital signs are growing weaker."

By then, we had nurses who cared for Dad round the clock. He had long ago been moved into the den on the first floor so he wouldn't have to climb the stairs, and now a nurse was always with him, checking his pulse, his blood pressure, his temperature. Even Hope knew what "vital signs" meant.

Mom called her parents in California, her brother and his family in Oregon, and Dad's aunt Laura in Vermont, and told them to fly in. (Dad didn't have any family left aside from his aunt.) She didn't have to call our neighbors or friends, though. They knew how things stood and had been dropping by regularly.

But they left us alone the next morning. I woke up early, Hope sleeping soundly beside me. Lately she'd been afraid to sleep alone in her room. Often I'd find her next to me when my alarm went off.

I left Hope in my bed and tiptoed downstairs. Mom was sitting in the kitchen, the lights off, sipping black coffee. She was wearing the same clothes she'd had on the day before.

"Mom?" I said.

"Morning, honey." Mom's voice was thick, her eyes red-rimmed.

"Were you up all night?" I asked.

Mom nodded. "So was Brent. He's still with Dad. Why don't you go sit with him?"

"Okay."

The light in the den was dim. The shades were up halfway, but outside the sky was still gray. Brent was sitting in a chair next to Dad's bed, tipped back so he was leaning against the wall. He was holding Dad's hand and staring out the window. The nurse was in the hall outside. She'd been giving us more and more time alone with Dad.

"Hi," I whispered to Brent. I sat down on the other side of the bed and picked up Dad's free hand. Dad was asleep sitting up, which was the only way he could breathe now.

Brent didn't answer me.

"Why don't you go sleep for a couple of hours?" I asked him.

Brent shook his head.

I knew why. He wanted to be with Dad at the very, very end, whenever that would be. So did I. At least, I thought I did.

So Brent and I sat.

Dad slept.

Mom came in. Carrie came in. Hope woke up crying and came in.

And still Dad slept.

I kept looking at his chest to see if he was breathing. He was, but his breathing was shallow and irregular.

The hours crept by.

At ten o'clock, Carrie said she had to go to the bathroom. She got halfway out the door of the den, then turned and came back. "It'll have to wait," she said. "I want to be here."

Mom sat in the rocker with Hope in her lap. They were both dozing. I moved to the end of the bed, and Carrie took my place next to Dad. Brent didn't budge.

At ten-thirty, the nurse came in and took Dad's blood

pressure. She felt for his pulse. Then she turned to leave.

"When?" Mom asked the nurse as she was closing the door.

"Soon."

Hope suddenly said sleepily that she had to throw up. The nurse took her so Mom could stay with Dad. She didn't bring Hope back for forty-five minutes. When she did, Hope had obviously been given a bath, was wearing fresh clothes, and had had her hair washed and brushed. She looked one hundred percent better. We'd been neglecting her a bit.

At noon Dad woke up. Sort of. His gaze traveled slowly around the room. After several seconds he said, "Are you all here?" His voice was so faint I could barely understand him. He closed his eyes again.

Mom stood up, set Hopie in the rocker, and sat on the bed. "We're all here," she said, leaning toward him.

Dad opened his eyes partway. "Tell the kids I love them," he said.

"They know that," Mom replied gently, her voice quavering. "They're right here."

Mom bent over and kissed Dad on the forehead. "And I love you."

Dad smiled faintly. Carrie let go of his hand, and he reached up to touch Mom's lips with his fingers. Then, abruptly, he fell asleep again.

He never woke up.

When the nurse came in a little while later, she felt for his pulse and couldn't find it. Swiftly she pulled out her stethoscope and listened to his chest. Then she forced his eyelids open and checked his eyes.

At last she turned to Mom and said, "He's gone."

I gasped, but Mom just nodded. She looked at us and said, "If you don't mind, I'd like some time alone with him."

"Okay," said Brent. He took Hopie by the hand and led her outside. Carrie and I followed.

The four of us huddled on the couch in the living room. Carrie began to cry softly and then to sob. Hope wriggled into my lap and began to cry, too. We tried to comfort each other, but none of us could say anything.

Presently, Mom came out of the den. "Brent?" she said. "Would you like to go in?"

Brent rose and went into the den, closing the door behind him. A few minutes later he came out and Carrie went in. I was still sitting on the couch hugging Hopie tightly. Mom began making phone calls in the kitchen.

When Carrie came out, she looked at me. "Liza?"

I shook my head.

"Don't you want to—"

"*No!*" There was no way I was going back into that room. Not alone, and not with anybody else. It was all right being with him when I thought he was alive, but I could not sit and talk with my dead father.

"It's all right, Liza," Mom said, coming back into the living room.

A few minutes later, people began arriving. Mrs.

Washburn came first, then a man from the funeral par-
lor. Then Denise's mother. Two doctors arrived. The
nurse left, but soon returned. Beth Perkins, Mom's
best friend, came. Mom's parents arrived. More relatives came.

I quickly lost track of who was in the house and
what time it was. I retreated to my room, feeling numb.
I don't know how long I stayed there. Three people
knocked on my door, and I told each of them that I
wanted to be alone. But when Denise walked in, I let
her stay. I was glad to see her. I didn't even know
school was over.

"How are you?" she asked.

I shrugged. "I feel like I did when Charlie was
killed."

"You're not going to let yourself cry, are you." It was
a statement, not a question.

"Denise, please don't—"

"I'm not kidding, Liza. Remember what I told you
when Charlie died?"

I nodded. "Not to put it off.... But I can't cry."

"Maybe not right now. But when you do feel like
crying, no matter what you think, it's a lot easier to cry
and let go of your father than to keep everything inside.
Okay?"

We sat for awhile, not saying anything, just being
together.

Denise stretched. "You know what my favorite memory of your father is?" She began to smile.

"What?" I asked.

"Actually, I have two. One is that time he tried out your skateboard. Remember?"

I began to smile, too. "He could hardly stay on it," I said. "He kept trying to go down the driveway and falling off. And then that one time he stayed on, he rode out into the street and almost hit that police car!"

"Yeah."

"What's the other memory?"

"It was right after my own father died. I was over here one day feeling pretty bad. I was moping around, and you didn't know what to do with me. I mean, we were little then. Anyway, your dad asked me what was wrong, and I said something like who was ever going to take me sledding again, and he said he'd be glad to. He said he knew he wouldn't be as good as my dad, but that he really wanted to take me."

"And he did take you, didn't he?" I said.

"Yup. Lots of times. You and Brent and Carrie would come, so it *wasn't* like when Dad and I used to go alone, but it was fun. That was when I started to see that maybe life would go on after all."

"Dad always knew the right thing to say. He always knew how people were feeling," I said.

"Yeah." Denise grabbed a Kleenex from the box on my dresser and began dabbing at her eyes. "First my father, then yours," she whispered.

I nodded. "Let's go downstairs," I said. "I better see how Hope's doing."

"Okay."

Denise and I put our arms around each other and

went down to the living room, which was full of people. We found Hope sitting rather uncomfortably in Grandpa's lap. Denise and I took her into the kitchen.

"How's your stomach?" I asked her.

"Fine."

"Are you sure?"

"It's hungry. It's rumbling."

"All right." I cut three slices from a pound cake I found on the counter. There was food everywhere. No one showed up empty-handed.

Hope and Denise and I sat at the table, picking at the cake.

"Some people took Daddy away," Hope commented.

"I know."

"He's dead, isn't he?"

"Yes, he is."

Hope stuffed a huge piece of cake in her mouth. "And I know what that means. Just like Charlie. He isn't coming back."

Chapter Two

A week later, there was a memorial service for Dad. It was held on the last day of school. Brent and Carrie and I had missed the entire last week and were going to make up the work and exams over the summer.

Dad had planned the memorial service himself. He'd decided where he wanted the service to take place, and he'd chosen the music to be played. He'd said he didn't want a eulogy, but he'd asked Mom, Brent, Carrie, Hope, and me each to read or recite something, if we wanted to. He'd asked Denise to play the piano. Dad had told us he wanted the service to be short and to remind people of his life, not of his death.

On a warm, sticky Tuesday morning Brent drove Mom, Hope, Carrie, and me to the Kimball Funeral Home, arriving an hour before the service was supposed to start. Denise came with us, clutching her music nervously. We parked in front of the home and

walked up a flagstone path, the scent of honeysuckle
and lush early-summer grass filling our noses. When
we opened the door, another heavy scent overcame
us—flowers. I've never seen so many. Mr. Kimball,
the director of the funeral home, said he'd never seen
so many either. Bouquet after bouquet sat on tables,
benches, chairs, and the floor in the receiving hall.
They just kept arriving. Mom asked Mr. Kimball to
give them to the Neuport Medical Center after the
service.

"But those are *our* flowers, Mommy," Hope whined.
"I want them."

Hope had a bad case of the "I wants." She'd had it
all week. She wanted everything—every note or tele-
gram that was delivered, a taste of all the food that
arrived. And she wouldn't throw anything away, not
even trash.

"Mo-ther," I'd complained more than once. I was
thoroughly exasperated with Hope.

"Honey," Mom said patiently, "she'll work through
this. Her father was just taken away from her. She
doesn't want to let go of anything else."

Mr. Kimball led us to the room where the service
would take place. It was big, with lots of pews in it,
but two teenagers were busily lining up folding chairs
wherever they could fit them.

"Judging by the number of flower arrangements that
are arriving," Mr. Kimball explained, "the service is
going to be heavily attended."

Mom went off with Mr. Kimball to discuss last-minute arrangements, and we kids sat in a little anteroom, waiting. The room was hot, even with the window open, and we didn't say much.

After a while, Brent noticed that people were starting to arrive. Soon cars lined both sides of the street in front of the funeral home. Others streamed up the drive to the parking lot in back.

"Hey," said Carrie at one point. "Look at that."

We crowded to the window to look out. Two black limousines with dark windows had paused in front of the home.

"Who do we know who's that rich?" I asked.

"It looks like gangsters," said Carrie, awed.

Doors started to open, and we could see feet stepping onto the pavement.

"If they're so rich, how come the chauffeurs aren't getting out and opening the doors for them?" asked Denise.

None of us knew. We continued to watch, mystified, as the people emerged from the limos.

"Oh, wow," said Brent suddenly. "You know who they are? They're from Dad's office in New York. There's his secretary, and there's Tina Crandall, and there's Mrs. Reit and Ben Sandford and Dad's boss."

"All the way from New York," I repeated.

"In limos," added Carrie.

"The company must have liked Dad an awful lot," I said.

"A lot of people did," said Brent.

The service was supposed to start at eleven o'clock. At ten minutes to eleven, Mom came into the room to wait with us and to tell Denise she could take her place at the piano. At eleven, Mr. Kimball stuck his head in to say that they were having trouble seating people and that the service would be delayed ten minutes. At eleven-fifteen, he said he needed five more minutes.

When the service finally started, every seat was taken, and more people were standing in the aisles and across the back of the room. The side door had been opened and about forty others stood patiently on the lawn trying to see in.

As Mom, Brent, Carrie, Hope and I walked through the crowded, silent room, I saw neighbors and relatives. I saw Dad's nurses from the hospital and several of his doctors. I saw friends of mine and friends of Brent's and friends of Carrie's. I saw our teachers and I saw Hopie's beloved Mrs. Harper from her school.

I had to swallow hard to keep from crying.

I don't remember much of what went on at the service, but I do remember that Denise played two pieces by Bach that were favorites of Dad's. Then Mom stood up and said something, but I don't remember what. Brent stood up next, turned to face the people, and recited "Mending Wall," a poem by Robert Frost that Dad had liked very much and had read over and over again.

Carrie stood next, but I don't remember what she said, just that it was something she read from a crumpled piece of notebook paper, and that by the time she finished it, anybody who hadn't already been crying, was crying.

After that, it was my turn, and when I stood I found that I didn't have much stage fright at all. In fact, I didn't need the index card full of notes that I was holding.

"What I want to say," I began, "is that if Dad had to die so soon, this is just the way he would have wanted it to happen. He had time to prepare for it, and he chose the way to spend his last months. Once he told me that sometimes sudden deaths are harder than lingering deaths because so much is left unsaid. Dad was grateful for these months because we were able to say things to each other, and to finish things up.

"Dad also said that this service is supposed to be a remembrance of his life, not of his death, so I want to tell you that Dad was a special father. He always listened, and had time for his kids."

There was at least another paragraph left to my speech, but I suddenly decided it was too personal, so I wound it up with, "I think we are all lucky to have known him."

Hope was next. We had told her several times that there were going to be a lot of people at the service and that she didn't have to say anything, but she was determined not to be left out. Now Brent stood and picked her up so everyone could see her. I wasn't sure what she was going to say. She'd been "rehearsing" at home, but she said something different every time.

"I miss my daddy," Hope began, and immediately started to cry. Brent handed her a tissue and she wiped her eyes. Then she seemed to be okay.

I watched her, safe in Brent's arms, fingering her gold locket as she spoke. She never once looked out at the people, and I don't think many of them heard her, but the ones in front sure did.

"He's a very nice man," Hope went on. "He's funny and he sings me funny songs. He calls me Emmy. No one else does."

At that point, Mom buried her face in her hands and wept silently.

"He likes animals, even Mouse, and he can always fix my swing. He's...he was a nice man," she said again. "He was tall. I love my daddy. That's all."

Brent put her down then. All around me I could hear sniffing and little gasps and hands rummaging through purses for more Kleenex. Carrie was crying rather loudly.

Denise struck a chord on the piano and played another piece. The service was over about fifteen minutes later.

Afterward, our family stood in the receiving room. Everyone wanted to talk to us on the way out. They wanted to hug us, too, and I kept pulling back. I didn't want all those arms around me.

"Dear," Mrs. Washburn said warmly, "I'm so sorry."

She drew me to her, and I stood stiffly and allowed her to kiss my cheek. Then I stepped back.

When Mrs. Petersen came up and put her arms out, I didn't move a muscle. She paused and I saw her glance at me, thoughtfully. Then she moved on and gave Mom a hug.

I noticed Hopie looking sort of woozy then, so I said to Denise, who was nearby, "Come on, let's get out of here." We took Hope back to the little anteroom, and she perked up when Denise handed her a piece of candy.

Later, there was a reception back at our house. Now I understood why everyone had brought food by all week—we could serve it to the guests. I spent most of the reception in the kitchen slicing cake and arranging plates of fruit and filling candy bowls.

Twice Mom came in and said she'd like me to join the guests, but I couldn't do it. They were all telling me to buck up and be brave and that things could only get better. And if I heard one more person tell Brent he was the man of the family now, I thought I'd scream—if Brent didn't kill the person first.

At last I escaped to my room. I locked the door, lay down on my bed, and felt the tears begin to fall. "Oh, no," I thought. "It's starting." I tried to turn off the tears, afraid that if I started crying, I'd never be able to stop. But I couldn't turn them off entirely. So I let myself cry for awhile and then went to my desk and found the copy of Dad's obituary that had appeared in the *Neuport News* the day before. Through eyes blurred with tears I read it once, then crumpled it up, took it into the bathroom, and set fire to it in the sink.

As I watched the flames slowly devour it, I suddenly felt very angry. "Dad, you jerk," I thought. "Why did you have to die? Why did you leave us without you?"

BOOK III

Autumn Again

Chapter One

On a Wednesday afternoon in the middle of November, I slammed my locker shut on the eighth-grade floor of Neuport Middle School and ran down the two flights of stairs to the sixth-grade floor. I peeked through the window into Carrie's classroom. Even though the last bell had rung, Ms. Saunders, Carrie's teacher, hadn't stopped teaching. She always made Carrie late, and that made me impatient.

I leaned against the wall, dropped my book bag on the floor, and waited.

It was exactly five months and twelve days since Dad had died. Summer had come and gone, and another autumn had arrived. It was just this time last year when Dad had first found out how sick he was. All we O'Hara kids were a year older. I was thirteen and Carrie was eleven. We were students at the same school again—for one year. Next year I would be a freshman in high school. It was hard to believe. And Brent was a senior in high school. Next year he'd be in college. That was even harder to believe.

Hopie was five. She'd turned five in September and had a big bash, inviting her entire class to her birthday party. She no longer went to the Harper Early Childhood Center. Now she went to the "extended kindergarten" program at the elementary school from 9:00 A.M. to 3:00 P.M. Hope wasn't thrilled with this turn of events. She'd loved Mrs. Harper (she'd even invited her to her birthday party), and she missed her old school. Kindergarten had not gotten off to a good start.

At last the door to Carrie's classroom opened and kids streamed out.

Carrie looked indignant. She didn't bother to greet me. "Do you know why Saunders was keeping us?" she asked huffily as we hurried out of the building. "Because," she went on without waiting for me to answer, "Tricia Kennedy said she didn't understand how to do an outline, so Saunders starts explaining the *whole thing*—to the *whole class*. Everyone *else* knows how to make an outline. Why should *we* get punished just because Tricia is practically retarded?"

"Carrie," I said, "it's okay."

"No, it's not. We're going to be late getting Sissy again. She'll probably be hysterical."

Carrie wasn't exaggerating. With Dad gone, money was tight. Since we couldn't afford day care for Hope anymore, Carrie and I were supposed to pick her up after school and take care of her until Mom came home.

Brent couldn't help us because he had a job after school and on weekends. He worked at Johnson's Garage, fixing cars, and made a lot of money, which was a good thing because he needed it to help pay for college. He needed a scholarship, too.

Anyway, even though Carrie and I had never once forgotten to pick up Hope, she seemed frightened that we would do just that. Sure enough, when we reached her classroom, Hopie was sitting on a rug in the story corner, hugging a teddy bear, sucking her thumb, and crying. Her teacher was hovering nearby, but I could tell that Hopie didn't want her to come any closer.

I couldn't understand it. Hope wasn't even the last kid left. Three others were still there, making a farm out of blocks. They looked perfectly happy. Hope looked as if she'd been abandoned. And she'd waited for someone to pick her up at the HECC nearly every day of her life.

We entered the classroom, and Carrie began gathering Hope's belongings while I spoke to Miss Donnelly, the teacher.

"How long has she been crying?" I asked.

"Just for a few minutes. She had a pretty good day today, but you know how it is. She thought you weren't coming."

I nodded. "All right."

"Don't worry," Miss Donnelly said. "She *is* improving. But this is a tough year for her, a lot of changes — new school, new house, your father gone."

The house. That was another thing. We'd had to

move out of 25 Bayberry. For me, the day Mom broke that news to us was almost as awful as the day she'd told us Dad was first in the hospital. The house was part of the family; it was O'Hara; it was *Dad*. Twenty-five Bayberry had been lived in by O'Haras for almost two hundred years. Selling the house had been like getting rid of the last of my father.

Even Dad's gentle aunt Laura, whom we rarely heard from, had stepped in when she found out Mom planned to sell. She'd tried to buy the house herself, just to keep it in the family, but she didn't have nearly enough money.

And that was the whole problem, of course. Neither did we.

We weren't poor or anything, but as I said, money was tight. With Dad gone, our income was cut by more than half. Plus Mom was now facing the first of four college tuitions. On top of that, insurance hadn't covered all of Dad's medical bills, and we owed thousands of dollars to the Neuport Medical Center and to the nursing service we'd used.

So one hot August evening, Mom had gathered us together and told us we were going to move. "This house is much too big and costly for us to keep," she'd said. "The yard is huge. Dad liked to take care of it, but I don't, and I don't want you kids to feel you have to. And a lawn service is too expensive. The heating bills here are sky-high, and the repairs on an old place like this are needed too often. Do you realize that in a couple of years, a new roof will have to be put on?

"I spoke to a real estate agent, and I've figured that with the money we'd make selling Twenty-five Bayberry, we can buy a new smaller home *and* pay all the hospital and nursing bills."

We'd protested, of course. I'd cried, and Brent had stormed off angrily, but Mom's reasoning was too logical, although selling the house wasn't easy for her either. The day we moved, she sat down on the last packing carton before the movers took it out of the house. "It's not fair," she said to me. "It's just not fair." And she burst into tears.

Moving day was in early September. The new house was a small one in a development just two streets away from Bayberry. It sat on a measly half-acre of land that was absolutely bare except for two twigs in the front yard which the real estate agent called maple trees.

At 25 Bayberry, which had rooms to spare, each of us had had our own bedroom. The new house had three bedrooms. Carrie and I shared one, Brent got one to himself since he was the only boy, and Mom and Hope shared one. Clearly, that was not an ideal arrangement. But Mom said that next year when Brent went away to college, I could have his room and Hope could move in with Carrie.

"Liza, we're ready." I turned away from Miss Donnelly to see Carrie holding a bundled-up Hope by the hand.

"Okay. Thanks, Miss Donnelly," I said. "Good-bye."

"Good-bye. . . . Good-bye, Hope."

Hope looked at Miss Donnelly, and for a second or

two I thought she wasn't going to answer her. But at
last she said, "'Bye."

"Show-and-Tell tomorrow, okay?" Miss Donnelly
reminded her.

"Okay."

We started the walk home.

"Are you going to bring something for Show-and-
Tell, Sissy?" Carrie asked her.

Hope was busy watching her breath puff along in
the frosty air. She thought for a moment. "Could I bring
Dr. J.?"

Dr. J. was our new kitten. He was named for Julius
Erving, the famous basketball player, because he liked
to leap through the air. Mom had brought Dr. J. home
shortly after we'd moved to the new house. She'd gotten him at the Pet Emergency Center where we'd taken
Charlie so many months ago. He was an eight-week-
old butterball then who looked just like Charlie, and
in fact, Mom had gotten him more for me than for
anyone else, but he didn't do the trick. He was cute
and cuddly, but he wasn't Charlie.

He slept with Hope every night.

"Oh, Hope, I don't think so," I said. "He'd have to
stay all day in your classroom. You'd have to bring his
food to school. And his litter box."

"Yeah," agreed Hope, sounding disappointed.

"What else could you bring?" I asked.

"I don't know. Nothing."

And that was the end of that conversation. I glanced
at Carrie, who shrugged.

When we reached our house, we were greeted noisily by Fifi, Mouse, and Dr. J., who all appeared to be starving. Fifi jumped up and down as I unlocked the front door and then skittered into the kitchen, feet sliding on the linoleum, Mouse and the Doctor at her feet.

Hope giggled. (The animals were among the few things that made her giggle these days.) Then she fed the pets while Carrie and I fixed the three of us a snack. After that we fooled around, and Denise and her sister, Maggie came over for awhile. When they left, it was time to start dinner. Brent and Mom got home from work around six o'clock, and soon we were sitting down to eat. It was a routine, and I liked it—knowing what was going to happen every hour of the day. No surprises.

Another thing I liked was dinner in the small dining room of our new house. I had thought I would hate it, after all the meals we'd eaten in the dining room of 25 Bayberry, with its high ceiling and brass chandeliers and the rose-patterned wallpaper that had covered the walls for almost eighty years. But the first time we sat down to eat in the new house, I felt relieved. It took several minutes for me to figure out why. Then I realized that the room was so cramped that we hardly missed Dad at all. During the last summer at 25 Bayberry, his absence had screamed out to us at every meal. In the new house, in the cramped quarters, the five of us seemed to fit around the table almost naturally. We looked more like a completed jigsaw puzzle and less like one with a piece missing.

At dinner that night, our conversation somehow turned to Christmas. I forget who started the discussion, but before long, I saw a familiar sparkle in Hope's eyes. She listened to Carrie and Brent talking about saving money for Christmas presents. After awhile she said, "Mommy, do you think we'll make things in Miss Donnelly's room?"

Mom looked confused. "What kinds of things, honey?"

"You know, *Christmas* things," Hope said impatiently.

"Like macaroni chains?" asked Carrie with a giggle.

Hope scowled at Carrie, then turned her attention back to Mom. "Like what we made with Mrs. Harper— snowmen and stars and snowflakes and a Santa Claus and presents." She was growing excited at the very thought of it all.

"I imagine so," said Mom.

"Goody," replied Hope. And then, "Goody, goody, *goody!*"

Mom, Brent, and Carrie were looking very pleased at this change in Hope, and they began making other Christmas plans, but I couldn't join in. Something numbing had washed over me. The idea of Christmas made me feel awfully sad. How could we celebrate Christmas this year? How could we do it without Dad? It didn't feel right. He'd want to be *with* us.

I put my fork down, unable to finish eating. Maybe we could sort of skip Christmas this year. Cancel it. It wasn't a terribly original idea, I knew. It had been done before. The Grinch tried it, and Ebenezer Scrooge would have loved it, but it seemed right for our family. We could ignore Christmas, or maybe just go out to dinner or pretend we were Buddhists or something.

I was about to suggest this to the others when the phone rang. Brent sprinted for it, listened for several seconds, then said disgustedly, "Liza, it's for you. Denise."

"Who were you expecting?" I demanded as I took the phone from him. "El-len?" Ellen Myers was Brent's new girlfriend.

Brent made a face and went back to the dining room.

"Denise?" I said.

"Hi!" Denise sounded as if she were bubbling over. "You'll never guess what. Never. So I'll just tell you."

"Okay," I said, and quietly closed the door between the kitchen and the dining room.

"Cathryn Lynn just called…"

"Yeah?"

"And you know how she sits next to Margie in your math class?"

"Yeah?"

"And Margie sits next to Marc Radlay?"

"Yeah?" I could feel my heart pounding faster.

"Well, today Margie told Cathryn Lynn that she overheard Marc telling Justin Sommerville that he likes you!"

"You're kidding!"

"No, I swear."

I couldn't believe it. For two years I'd been wanting a boyfriend. Now, without my doing a single thing, *Marc Radlay* was practically falling in my lap. Maybe. I wondered why he hadn't said anything to me. We had two classes together, plus lunch and free period, and he never spoke to me. He always hung around with Justin and a bunch of other eighth-grade boys.

"What should I do?" I whispered frantically to Denise.

"Nothing," she said. "Just wait. And wear the makeup I gave you."

"Okay..."

"Listen, I have to go."

"Okay.... 'Bye...."

"See you tomorrow."

I hung up the phone in a daze. Marc Radlay liked me. He liked *me!*

Chapter Two

I stood in the kitchen for a few seconds, trying to put Marc Radlay out of my head. After the initial shock and excitement, I suddenly wasn't sure how I felt about the news. Liking a girl meant asking her to be your girlfriend...didn't it? And being someone's girlfriend meant going out and having fun. That was what was holding me back. Fun. I hadn't had much of it since Dad died, and I didn't think I wanted any of it now.

I returned to the dining room and sat down. The topic of conversation had changed. While I was relieved that we were not talking about Christmas anymore, I wasn't thrilled with the new topic. It was money. That was all we seemed to talk about these days. How we could get more money, and how we could stretch what we had. At the moment, Brent was on one of my least favorite money subjects.

"But what if I don't win the scholarship?" he was saying.

"We'll worry about that if it happens," replied Mom. "For now, just keep your grades—"

"I think we *should* worry about it now," interrupted Brent. "If we wait until it happens, I won't be able to go to Princeton. I'll have to go somewhere else. It's not like someone is going to hand me the money on a silver platter if I don't get the scholarship. It's either get the scholarship or no Princeton."

"Princeton," said my mother, "is not the only good school in the country."

"I know," said Brent, "but it's the one I want to go to. And all the other good schools are just as expensive."

Mom sighed. "Brent, go ahead and apply to the state university, in case. Anyway, there's still *some* money put aside for you—we didn't spend *every*thing in the college account—and I'm looking into loans. You're saving money this year, too, and there are work programs at most universities. I hope you're investigating them."

"I am."

A lot was being left unsaid, but I could hear it all anyway. All the "buts" and "ands" and "what ifs." I really thought Brent was worrying unnecessarily. In the first place, his grades were excellent; he had a good shot at being valedictorian of his class. In the second place, it wasn't as if there was just *one* scholarship he could win. Lots of scholarships and prizes were awarded to students in our town every spring.

But Brent, once he had understood just how tight money was, had taken over the worry of it as a sort of pet project. He had encouraged Mom to cut back on our allowances, to buy the cheapest brands at the grocery store, to trim our hair herself instead of taking us to the hair salon, to save on gas, and that sort of thing. He'd even told Mom not to adopt Dr. J. because he said we didn't need another mouth to feed.

"Well," Brent continued, just when I thought we were through talking about money, "maybe we could cut back some more. I could sell my car. And why do we need two color TVs? We could sell one easily."

"Brent," said Mom warningly.

"And what are you going to do next year when I'm gone?"

Carrie snorted. "We'll have fun," she replied. "Waste stuff right and left. Go all out for Skippy peanut butter. Buy toilet paper without checking to see how many sheets come on the roll. Maybe we'll splurge and"— she paused dramatically and went on in a stage whisper—"go to a *movie*."

Hope and I smiled. Mom hid her own smile and said mildly, "Okay, that's enough, Carrie."

Brent glared at Carrie. I could almost see a four-letter word forming on his lips, but he bit it back.

An awkward silence followed. Hope, that familiar gleam in her eyes once again, glanced around the table and filled the silence by saying, "Let's talk about Christmas some more, okay? Let's—"

"Let's not," I snapped. It was the first thing I'd said since I sat down. Everyone looked at me. "I don't think we should even have Christmas this year. I don't see how we can. It's not fair." I tried to calm down and sound more reasonable.

"But Christmas always comes, doesn't it?" asked Hope nervously.

"That's right. It always does," Mom assured her.

"Well, I think the O'Haras should just... skip it this year."

"Why?" asked Hope.

"Yeah, why?" said Carrie.

Brent was looking at me as if I were crazy. Even he, the miser, wanted Christmas, a low-cost Christmas, but Christmas nevertheless.

"Why?" I repeated. How was I going to explain this one? "Because... because Dad liked it so much and now he's gone. It just doesn't seem fair to have it without him, to make him miss it."

"Don't you think Dad would want *us* to celebrate Christmas?" asked Mom. "Of all people, he would know best what fun it is. I don't think he'd want his family to miss out on something so special. Particularly after the year we've had."

"Oh, *Mom*," I said. "Who knows *what* Dad would have wanted? Ever since June, people have been saying, 'Your father would have wanted it this way. Your father would have done this, your father would have done that.'"

"Well, then," Mom broke in, "how do you know Dad

would want us *not* to celebrate Christmas?"

"Yeah!" said Carrie triumphantly.

"Carrie, shut up."

"Liza, go to your room this instant."

I stared at Mom. It was the first time she'd ever sent me to my room.

"And that's another thing," I said, my voice shaking. "It's not even my room. I have to share it with *her*." I pointed at Carrie. "I don't have any privacy anymore."

"You're not the only one," Mom replied tightly. "Now leave the table. I'll talk to you later. Carrie, you can do your homework in the kitchen tonight, so Liza can have a little space."

I climbed the stairs slowly, the sound of Carrie's noisy protests dying behind me.

When a knock came on the door about a half an hour later, I didn't bother to answer it. I knew it was Mom, and I knew she would let herself in anyway.

It was and she did.

I was already in bed. The thought of curling up in a flannel nightgown had seemed very appealing. Fifi was at my feet, sprawled across the patchwork quilt, snoring gently.

"Liza," Mom said, "I've been thinking. Certainly you have the right to voice your opinion on this subject, and you have the right to your thoughts. But you do not have the right to *inflict* your ideas on everyone else. Do you understand me? You may do whatever you want about Christmas this year, but the rest of us are going to celebrate it, and I want us to be able to do that without any interference. Okay?"

I was lying on my stomach, facing the wall. I nodded.

"I want to point out," said Mom, "that Christmas is the first thing that has begun to pull Hope out of her depression."

I rolled over and looked at Mom.

"Yes, depression," she repeated, sensing my unasked question. "Children can suffer from depression just as adults can. And whether you know it or not, Hope has been terrified by the things that have happened this year. She may be smart, but she doesn't really understand why anything happened. She knows Dad isn't coming back, she knows this is her new home, she knows Miss Donnelly is her new teacher, but she doesn't understand why. I think what she sees now is that life isn't stable or predictable. As far as she's concerned, the rest of us could be taken from her just as easily as her father was. And that scares her. She needs to know that there *is* some predictability to her life. That's one reason she's so excited about Christmas. She wants it to come just like it did last year. She wants us to celebrate it like we did last year.... Can you understand that?"

"But it won't be like last year," I whispered. "Dad won't be with us."

Mom smoothed back my hair, brushing it from my forehead. "I know, sweetheart. And we all miss him. We'll especially miss him at Christmas. But our lives have to go on."

"It still doesn't seem right."

"Not to you, maybe, and that's fine. That's your feeling."

"You're still going to celebrate Christmas this year?"

"Yes, of course."

"Well, I'm really not going to celebrate with you."

"All right. I understand. I don't agree with what you're doing, but I understand it. If you change your mind, the rest of us will be pleased to have you join in."

I sighed. "Okay."

"I'll go talk to the other kids now."

Mom left the room and closed the door behind her. A little while later, Carrie came in. "I haven't finished my homework," she told me. "You can have our room until I'm done."

"Really?" I asked. I was glad she hadn't mentioned Christmas.

"Sure. I'll leave the door closed, too, if you want."

"Thanks, Carrie," I said. Some privacy was just what I needed.

Chapter Three

The room I shared with Carrie was very different from the room I'd had at 25 Bayberry. For one thing, of course, it was crowded. It was smaller than my old bedroom and had the furniture and belongings of two people stuffed into it: two beds (we had vetoed the idea of a double-decker), two dressers, two bookcases, an armchair, my desk (there was no room for Carrie's desk, but she didn't seem to mind), Carrie's board games and stuffed animals, and my tape deck and collections of sea shells and china cats.

In my old room, a bulletin board had hung over my desk. In the new house, the desk was under a window and there was no available wall space anyway, what with the closet, the other window, the wall lamps, and Carrie's kitten posters.

I sat down at my desk, absent-mindedly opened a drawer, saw a photo of Dad, and quickly shut the drawer. It wasn't easy to look at pictures of Dad. Mom said she thought it was good to look at old photos of him. It would help us to remember him as he was when he was healthy—to remember him smiling or fooling around or working in the yard. But I had a hard time remembering him any way except the way he was the day he died.

"That's gross," Carrie had said when I confided it to her one night. "It's—what do you call it? It's morbid."

"I can't help it," I replied.

And I couldn't. I mean, how many people are sitting right next to their father when he dies? When his last breath leaves his body?

Dad was buried in a little cemetery behind the oldest church in Neuport. We didn't go to that church, but so many past generations of O'Haras were buried there that Dad had thought he should be, too. All in the family. Ha, ha.

I hadn't been to see the grave. Everyone else had been—regularly. Even Hope. Sometimes they took flowers. (More than once I'd seen Hope go off with a bouquet of wilted dandelions.) Sometimes they watered the grass around the headstone. Sometimes one would go alone, without anything. And stay a long time. Why, I wasn't sure.

"You should come," said Carrie.

"No way," I said. "It's not even *him* buried there. It's not his body; it's just a little pot full of ashes."

Ashes had become something of a problem for me.

I saw ashes and I thought of death. It started, not the first time I saw the pot in the funeral home, but later, that time when I burned my father's obituary. I looked at the ashes as the tapwater washed them down the drain, and I kept thinking, "They're like flakes of Dad, flakes of Dad, flakes of Dad."

I knew it was weird, but I couldn't help it. Now I got nervous if a smoker came to the house. I couldn't rinse out the dirty ashtrays. I wouldn't sit in the living room if there was a fire in the fireplace. Flakes of Dad, flakes of Dad. No one knew about the ashes thing. I was too embarrassed to talk about it.

"What do you *do* at the cemetery?" I asked Carrie one day when she returned from a rather long visit.

"I talk to him."

"To Dad?"

"Yeah."

"You're kidding."

"No, Liza," she said after an uncomfortable pause, "I'm not kidding."

"Sorry. It's just that it's..."

"That it's what? Strange? You haven't been there once. I think *that's* strange."

Well, maybe it was. But what I thought was *really* strange was the way the rest of the family were just going on about their lives. It was almost as if Dad hadn't died—or hadn't existed. Mom was working harder than ever and was taking a course in educational administration at the community college. Brent was frantically applying to colleges and was doing a

million other things—working on the yearbook, seeing
Ellen, fiddling around with the insides of his car, playing football, and planning for Homecoming. Carrie was
just as bad. She had joined an art club at school, was
doing a lot of baby-sitting, and was thinking about
going out for the middle school's intramural basketball
team. How could they just pick up and go on like this?
It wasn't right. They didn't have any respect for Dad.

As for me, Dad was nearly the only thing I could
think about. At least once a day I thought I saw him
somewhere. One morning in school, for instance, I had
turned the bend in the staircase between the third
floor and the second floor, and in the crowd of people
coming up the stairs toward me was a tall man with
graying brown hair who was wearing tortoise-shell
glasses. "Dad!" I had nearly cried out, but almost immediately I saw that it was Mr. Yolen, one of the
seventh-grade history teachers.

Sometimes I fantasized that Dad hadn't really died.
It had all been an elaborate government plan for him
to escape from our family and his own past and to
assume a new identity. Everyone had been in on it—
the doctors, the private nurse, the men who took him
away. It all made sense, really. I mean, none of us
sitting around Dad's bed that last day had been aware
of his actual dying. We only knew that the nurse came
in, took his pulse, and announced that he was gone.
Which, all along, I'd thought was weird. Weren't you
supposed to know? Wasn't there supposed to be a death
rattle or a tremor or a gasp? Pretty weird. Sometimes

I could convince myself that this was true. The government had brainwashed Dad so he would go along with the scheme. Now Dad was walking around somewhere, healthy as a horse, under the assumed name of Bond—James Bond—or something.

Another thing. Dad's birthday was August 15, and it had come and gone last summer almost like any other day. We were still living at 25 Bayberry then. I had woken up late and come downstairs in my nightgown. Mom and Brent were on the porch in back of the house, drinking coffee. I sat down with them and propped my bare feet up on the railing.

"Morning, sweetie," Mom had said. "There's a slice of cantaloupe in the refrigerator for you."

"Oh, thanks."

"Want to go swimming with me today?" Brent had asked. "Jeff's asking a bunch of people over to break in the new pool."

"Sure.... Well, maybe."

Not a word about Dad's birthday. On that day the year before, we'd gotten up early, packed a picnic (complete with a birthday cake), and spent the day at the beach.

If I'd had the nerve, I would at least have gone to Dad's grave with some flowers. As it was, only Mom did that. Brent went to Jeff's party, and Carrie babysat for Susie and Mandy White all afternoon. Hope didn't know when Dad's birthday was, so she didn't matter.

Late in the afternoon, when Mom came back from

the cemetery, I saw her standing out in one of the flower gardens (Dad's favorite) crying, so I knew she was thinking about the day. But I'd thought we should observe it somehow, I mean, aside from going to his grave. So I wrote a poem about him and held a private moment of silence.

I looked out the window and sighed. I didn't like the view from the new house nearly as much as the one from 25 Bayberry. There were street lamps and phone poles everywhere. This time last year, looking out my bedroom window, I'd seen trees and a faded lawn and a little early snow. This time last year, Charlie had been alive. This time last year, Dad had been alive. And this time last year, we'd been about to start getting ready for our last Christmas together.

Chapter Four

The day after I decided to try to cancel Christmas, I happened to be gazing around the room instead of at the blackboard in math class. Ms. Pressman was at the board with her pointer, spearing a large X between two chalk lines and saying something about "the numerical value of a negative integer without regard to its sign," and I was feeling as blank as the rest of the kids in the class looked. My eyes wandered slowly to the left, and when I became aware of what was in front of them, I realized I was staring right into the eyes of Marc Radlay.

It was as if our eyes were locked. I suddenly went numb and sort of tingly all over, and my breath began to come in shallow little gasps, but I could *not* take my gaze away from Marc's.

Apparently, he couldn't shift his gaze, either. The next thing I knew, he was flashing a quick, tentative smile at me. He managed, somehow, in those two or three seconds, to look shy, sweet, amused, and nervous about Ms. Pressman—all at the same time.

I didn't have a chance to smile back, though, because just then Ms. Pressman's voice rose to a crescendo. "...the magnitude of a *quan*tity!" she cried, and everyone jerked to attention.

After that, I tried to stick with what she was saying, but my eyes kept drifting four seats over to Marc's profile. I studied the way his hair, which was a soft brown, curled over the top of his ear. I studied the freckles sprinkled across his nose and right cheekbone. I watched with great interest as he scribbled a note on a piece of paper from his assignment pad, put his hands inside his desk to fold it up, and passed the note to Justin Sommerville. And I watched with a fascination that bordered on horror as Marc, evidently in response to the note he'd gotten back from Justin, scribbled a second note, and passed it to Margie, who passed it to Cathryn Lynn—who passed it to me.

I couldn't believe it. No boy had ever passed *me* a note. I looked again at the wad of paper in my hand. Sure enough, it said LIZA across it in clear letters. I hid it inside my desk. Then I glanced to the left. Margie and Cathryn Lynn were grinning at me, but Marc was looking stiffly ahead, and I noticed that his ears were burning a bright red.

Margie began signaling frantically and mouthing at me to "Open it! Open it!"

As soon as Ms. Pressman turned her back to write

on the board, I opened the note. I had to do it slowly to keep it from crinkling. When at last it was unfolded, I read the words, feeling as if every eye in the room was on me instead of on Ms. Pressman. "Meet me on the playground after lunch," the note said. "I'll be waiting by the water fountain. Marc."

Heart pounding, I folded the note back up, and sneaked a look at Marc. He happened to be sneaking a look at me, so I nodded my head slightly to let him know I'd gotten the note and everything was okay.

He, Justin, Cathryn Lynn, and Margie *all* seemed to breathe sighs of relief, but no one was more relieved than I when a few minutes later, the bell rang.

I made a beeline for Denise's locker and found her standing in front of it, stuffing her gym clothes between some piano books and a pair of boots.

"Denise!" I whispered desperately, looking over my shoulder as if Marc might have followed me or something. "Look at this!"

My hands trembled as I fumbled for the note and shoved it at her.

She slammed her locker door, then unfolded the note. "Meet me on the playground after lunch," she read aloud.

"*Shhh!*"

"Liza, calm down." Denise went back to the note. "I'll be waiting by the water fountain. Marc." She paused. "Marc? *Marc?* Marc *Rad*lay? Oh, Liza! I told you, I told you! Didn't I tell you?"

"Yes!" We were both squealing and jumping up and

down. "How am I going to wait until fifth period? I'll never make it."

"I know," Denise said sympathetically.

I thought of something. "Oh, no! What am I going to say to him? Do you think he has something to tell me, or do you think he just wants to talk? If he just wants to talk, what do you think he wants to talk about?"

"I don't know," replied Denise. "Maybe—"

"Oh, no!" I cried again. "Look at how I'm dressed. How do I look?"

"You look fine. Makeup always improves your—"

The bell rang, signaling the start of fourth period.

"Oh, no, now we're late!"

Denise and I ran down the hall in opposite directions.

At the beginning of fifth period I met Denise at our usual table in the cafeteria. Margie and Cathryn Lynn joined us. We had brought our lunches because Thursday was usually ravioli and Jello-O day, and we all agreed that it was too disgusting to look at, let alone eat.

As soon as we had spread out our food and I had traded Cathryn Lynn my apple for her chocolate-chip cookies and Denise had traded Margie her potato chips for a cinnamon doughnut, I looked around the cafeteria and said, "Where's Marc? He didn't say what time to meet him."

"Probably just whenever you're done eating," said Denise.

"Yeah, but I don't want to make him wait. And I don't want to get there first."

Cathryn Lynn elbowed me. "There he is!" she whispered loudly. "Now you can watch him to see when he leaves the cafeteria."

I looked across the room, and sure enough, there was Marc with Justin and some other boys. As I was watching him, he looked up and saw me. We both blushed and went back to our lunches.

Ten minutes later, I was finished eating. Marc was still at his table.

"Well, now what?" I said, panicking.

"Just wait for him to leave," said Margie.

"Are you guys *sure* I look all right?"

"You look great," said Cathryn Lynn. "Really."

Just then, Marc scrunched up his lunch bag, tossed it in a garbage can, and strode out the side door of the cafeteria onto the playground.

"Ohhhh..." I said.

"All right," said Denise. "Now don't do anything cute. Just be yourself."

"Myself! Who's myself?"

"And don't stammer," said Margie.

"I don't stammer."

"And don't let any long pauses get into the conversation," said Cathryn Lynn. "If he's not talking, then you talk."

I laughed nervously. "For all I know, he just needs the history assignment or something."

"I doubt it," said Denise. "Now brush your hair."

I opened my purse, pulled out a brush, and fixed my hair. Then I held a mirror up to my mouth to make sure I didn't have anything stuck between my teeth.

"Okay, go on," said Margie.

"Wish me luck."

"Good luck," said Denise and Margie and Cathryn Lynn at the same time.

I threw my lunch bag out and walked onto the playground. Our playground isn't actually a playground. It's more of a cement yard. The school officials had decided that junior high school students were too old for a playground, but not too old to need some outdoor place to use during school hours. Their compromise had been a very nice athletic field for gym classes and sports, and this cement yard for recess.

I saw Marc by the water fountain and headed over to him, my heart hammering away in my chest.

"Hi," I said brightly.

"Hi," said Marc.

I smiled at him.

He smiled back.

"Well," I said, and giggled.

Marc cleared his throat. "Well." He paused. "What I wanted to say, I mean, what I wanted to ask you is, see, there's this party coming up. Justin's parents are letting him give a big party, the kind where you stay for dinner and stuff. And he told me I could invite some kids to it, too, so I was wondering if you'd like to go to the party."

"Oh! Wow!" I said. I tried to sound excited, but

suddenly I felt as if I were a balloon that had just been pricked and all the air was slowly leaking out of me. There was no way Marc could have known how I felt about big parties—that I hated the crowded rooms and the noise. It was part of my stage fright. And there was certainly no way he could have known that I felt guilty about having too much fun—I mean, since Dad had died. Why couldn't Marc simply have asked me if I wanted to go to the library with him, or take a walk in the woods or something?

I didn't know what to say. I didn't want to ruin things with Marc, but there was no way I was going to go to a big party.

"That sounds neat!" I managed to appear reasonably excited. "Um, do you know what day the party is? I'll have to...have to check with my mother."

"Oh, sure," said Marc. "It's the Saturday after Thanksgiving."

"Great," I replied. "I'll let you know tomorrow, okay?"

"Okay! Meet me here, same time."

"All right." I cringed. Marc sounded really happy. And tomorrow I was going to let him down.

I smiled at him again. "Well...see you tomorrow."

"Yeah! See you!" Marc sauntered over to Justin and their friends, who were standing around a tetherball pole.

Just as Marc left, a big bunch of sixth-graders came running onto the playground, Carrie among them. Their playground schedule somehow overlapped with ours.

Suddenly, I felt very relieved that Carrie hadn't seen me with Marc.

I ran by her, calling hello, and went inside to find Denise.

Chapter Five

The next day, Marc and I met during recess as we had planned. I was a lot less nervous than the day before. I was also feeling like a rat.

"Hi, Liza!" Marc called as I approached him.

"Hi."

"Did you ask your mom?"

"Yeah, and . . . and I can't go to the party," I lied.

"Oh. Well, that's okay. Really," Marc said quickly.

"See, it's just because we're going to be out of town. We're going to spend Thanksgiving with these friends of Mom's, the Werners, who live in New Hampshire." This much was true. However, we were coming back on Friday. "We're not coming back until Saturday night," I told Marc, surprised at how easy it was to tell lies.

Marc brightened somewhat when he heard why I wasn't able to go to the party. You couldn't argue with being out of town. "Well," he said. "Listen, there's this funny movie at the Twin Theatre. It's not new, but it's really good. It's called *Airplane*. Have you ever seen it?"

"I don't think so," I said.

"Well, you have to! It's so funny. This guy keeps saying to this other guy, 'Surely you don't mean...' and the other guy keeps saying, 'Yes, I do, and don't call me Shirley!'"

I couldn't help laughing.

"You *have* to see it. Can you go tomorrow night?"

I thought quickly. The movie sounded like fun, too much fun. "Oh, gee. I just remembered. Tomorrow is Saturday, right? We're having company tomorrow night."

I looked across the playground to see Carrie's class being let loose. Carrie saw me at the same time, and her eyes widened when she realized I was talking to a boy. She wandered toward me and sat down on a stone bench, pretending to read a library book. I knew she was pretending because the book was called *All About Integers*.

"Mom said we have to be home for the company," I went on, trying to lower my voice enough so that Carrie couldn't hear me.

But Marc had no idea what was going on, and he was determined to go out with me. So he didn't lower *his* voice. "What about next weekend?" he asked. Then he remembered. "Oh, next weekend is Thanksgiving. But you're coming home on Saturday, right? So let's go Sunday afternoon, okay? We can go early."

Marc looked so eager that I just couldn't let him down again. "I'll check with my Mom, okay? I'll let you know on Monday."

"Great!" said Marc. "Hey, have you seen that new video?"

"Which one?" I asked.

Marc described it to me, and we started talking. We talked until the bell rang. As we walked inside together, I realized we'd been talking for almost twenty minutes. I couldn't believe it! It hadn't been awkward at all.

At dinner that evening, Carrie didn't even wait until everyone had been served before she opened her big mouth.

"Did you ask Mom yet?" she said, her eyes dancing.

"Ask Mom what?" said Mom suspiciously.

"Whether she can go to the movies with a boy. This boy in eighth grade, Marc Radlay, asked Liza to go to the movies with him. Oh, I'd just *die* if a boy asked *me!*" said Carrie rapturously. "I think that's so exciting."

I shot Carrie a look that, if she'd known any better, she would have interpreted as lethal. But she was too caught up in the fantasy—*my* fantasy—to pay attention.

"Liza, what's this all about?" asked Mom, amused.

"Oh, it's nothing."

"It doesn't sound like nothing. Come on, tell us."

"Do you have a boyfriend?" Hopie asked me curiously.

"No, Sissy!" I said, and giggled.

"But a boy asked you for a date?" said Mom.

"No. Just to the movies."

"Sounds like a date to me," said Brent.

"It would."

"Liza!" Mom laughed. "For heaven's sake. This is wonderful news. It doesn't really matter whether it's a real date. What movie are you going to see?"

"You mean I can go?"

"Of course," replied Mom. "You're thirteen years old. That's old enough to go to the movies with a boy."

"We're going to see *Airplane*," I said slowly. Now how had I gotten into this? Carrie. It was all her fault. I bet if *I'd* asked Mom if I could go, she'd have thrown a fit, and said that thirteen was too young to be going off with boys.

"What are you going to wear?" asked Mom.

"I don't know. Jeans, I guess."

"Jeans! Don't you want to look a little nicer than that? Maybe you need some new clothes."

"New clothes!" Brent jumped up. You'd have thought someone had just suggested that we buy a jet airplane for personal use. "Liza and Carrie have enough things hanging in their closet to clothe the entire population of Neuport—twice."

"We do not," cried Carrie. "Half of the stuff doesn't fit. It's waiting to be hand-me-downs for Hope, but *we* have to keep it in *our* closet because *Mom's* closet is all cramped up with her clothes and Hope's clothes. The rest of the stuff in our closet is—"

"—in perfectly good condition," Brent finished smugly.

"It is not. It's—"

"Enough!" shouted Mom.

"Yeah. You want Santa Claus to come or not?" threatened Hopie.

Everybody burst out laughing then, and Marc was forgotten.

At least until bedtime. At ten o'clock, Mom came into our room to say good night to Carrie and me. She sat on the edge of my bed and said, "You're really growing up, sweetheart." (I didn't feel grown up.) "If you do want a new sweater or something to wear to the movie, just tell me. I'm sure we can squeeze it out of Brent's budget."

"Only if you can squeeze water out of a stone," I said.

Mom smiled, then leaned over to kiss my forehead. "Good night, Lize."

"Night, Mom."

Mom kissed Carrie. "See you two in the morning."

As soon as she had closed the door, I whispered, "And from now on, butt *out* of my business."

"Huh?" said Carrie.

"You opened your big fat mouth. What'd you have to go and tell Mom about Marc for?"

Carrie sounded shocked. "Well, you were going to ask her about the movie yourself. You said so."

"And how do you know that? I thought you were so interested in the fascinating world of integers."

Even in the dark I could tell Carrie was blushing. "I don't know what you're so upset about," she said finally.

"Just stay out of my business, that's all."

"O-*kay!*"

"Okay."

Marc didn't wait until Monday to find out whether we could go to the movies. He called me at home on Saturday morning. Unfortunately, Carrie answered the phone. "Hello, this is Carrie O'Hara speaking. Who is this please?" she answered mechanically.

I was in the kitchen feeding Fifi, Mouse, and Dr. J. When Carrie heard who was calling, she clapped her hand over the mouthpiece and whispered as loudly as possible, "Liza! It's *him!* It's Marc!"

I dropped a can of cat food in the sink. All the animals jumped.

"You're kidding," I said.

Carrie shook her head slowly.

I took the phone from her. "Could I have a little privacy, please?" I whispered.

"Sure, sure." She left the kitchen. But I had a feeling she didn't go very far.

"Hello?" I said. Marc was the first boy I'd ever spoken to on the phone. Except for Brent and his friends. And Dad, if he counted as a boy.

"Hi, it's Marc. I was just wondering what your Mom

said about the movies. Can you go?"

I felt trapped. I hadn't decided what to do. "I—I
haven't exactly asked her yet," I lied. "She's been in
a really bad mood lately."

"Oh. Well, when you do ask her, ask if you can go
to Burger King with me afterward, okay?"

"Sure...."

Marc could have gotten more enthusiasm from a fish.
Still, it was sort of flattering.

"See you on Monday," said Marc.

"Okay...and thanks. 'Bye, Marc."

Marc hung up the phone, but I didn't. I depressed
the button, then lifted it and immediately dialed Denise. "Can you come over?" I asked her urgently. "Better yet, can I come over there? I need the privacy of
your room. I have to talk to you." I paused, then turned
away from the phone and yelled, "Carrie, get out of
here!" A shadow in the hall outside the kitchen dis-
appeared.

"Liza?" Denise said. "I'm sorry, I have a piano lesson this morning. What's going on? Can we talk over
the phone?"

"Not really. I don't know....Denise, after your father died, did you feel guilty about things? Like when
my dad would take you sledding and you'd have fun,
did you feel guilty afterward?"

"Oh, wow. You know, I don't think so, but I don't
really remember. It's beginning to fade."

"What is?"

"The whole thing. His death, the funeral, how sad I felt."

"Oh." How could something like that *fade?* How could someone forget the death of her own father? "Well, thanks," I said. "You better get to your lesson. I'll talk to you later."

As soon as we hung up, Mom came into the kitchen with her pocketbook. "Okay. How about some shopping? I was thinking that if you got a pair of white corduroys to wear with your blue and white Fair Isle sweater, you'd have a pretty nice outfit. And it would be casual enough for the movies. How does that sound?"

"Mom, that's great, but I really don't need any new clothes."

"Oh, come on, honey. We can have a treat every now and then."

"Well ... all right. Thanks."

Mom and I had a nice time shopping. She asked Carrie to stay home with Hope so the two of us could go off on our own. I tried to forget about Dad, and I managed for a little while. But when I got home and stood in front of the mirror wearing the new outfit and thinking about what it was for, this dreadful guilty feeling came over me, and suddenly I knew what I had to do.

On Monday, I caught Marc in the hall after math class and said, "I'm really sorry. I asked my mom, but she was still in a bad mood, and she said no."

Marc stared at me with a funny expression on his face. "Okay," he said, and walked away.

That evening when Mom got home from work and our family was in the kitchen getting ready for supper, she said, "Countdown. Six days until your first date!" It *wasn't* a date, but Mom wouldn't stop calling it that.

I flushed. "I have to tell you something," I said, trying to sound terribly disappointed. "Um, Marc broke our—our date today."

"Broke it! Why?" cried Mom.

"What a rat!" exclaimed Carrie.

"Take the pants back," said Brent.

"I don't know why," I said. "He just broke it."

Now I felt guilty for lying to Marc and guilty for lying to my family, but somehow, it wasn't as bad as the guilt I would have felt over Dad. I could do something about Marc and my family. I could fix things up. But there was nothing I could do about the guilt over Dad.

Chapter Six

Just before Thanksgiving vacation began, two things happened. My family suddenly seemed to plunge into Christmas preparations, and Denise caught me in my lie to Marc (the first lie, that is). Tuesday and Wednesday were days I'd rather forget, and they led to two weeks I'd rather forget.

Denise called me after school on Tuesday since I'd been trying to avoid her and hadn't seen much of her. I'd had a feeling she'd hear about the party sooner or later. But I wasn't expecting what she told me.

"Liza!" she cried.

Inwardly, I groaned. I wasn't prepared to talk about Marc.

"Guess what! Guess what!" she cried.

"What?" She didn't sound like someone who was going to accuse me of lying.

"I almost don't know how to say this, but Justin's

having a party on Saturday, and he asked *me* to it!"

"Hey! That's great!" I exclaimed. I meant it. I was thinking about Denise's reluctance to have boyfriends or consider marriage.

"Yeah! So Marc asked you to go, right? I mean I figured he did, since he's inviting people, too."

"Well, actually, I'm not going."

"You're *not!* Didn't he ask you?"

I paused, wondering whether to start some other lie, and decided against it. The last time I'd lied to Denise was when my father was first in the hospital and I told her it wasn't anything serious. "Yeah, he asked me, but I told him we're not coming back from the Werners' until Saturday night."

"How come? I mean, why did you say that? You'll be home on Friday, right?"

"Yeah. Oh, Denise, I don't know. I just don't want to go."

"But Liza, all I've been hearing from you for the last two years is how you wish you had a boyfriend. Then you had that crush on Marc when you were in *A Christmas Carol*—I know you did. Now Marc asks you to this big party, and you won't go. I don't get it.... And I think that's an awful thing to do to Marc. Lying to him."

"I know."

"Then why'd you do it?"

"Denise, lay off. I can't explain it." I think if she hadn't sounded so accusing, I might have tried to explain again, but not when she was in this mood. And particularly not if she was letting the death of her father fade away into unimportance.

That was our first major fight. We didn't make up until after school the next day. Carrie had gone to an art club meeting, so Denise came with me to pick up Hopie.

"I still think what you did was mean," she said, "but I don't want us to be mad at each other."

"Me neither," I said.

"I had thought it would be so much fun if you and I started sort of hanging out with Justin and Marc. I thought we could go to the movies together and stuff. Does this mean you don't want to see Marc? You don't want to go to movies or school games with him or anything?"

"Oh—" I had started to say, "Oh, *no!*" and then realized I wasn't sure. *Was* I going to hang around with Marc? Could I figure out something interesting for us to do that wouldn't be much fun?

We reached the elementary school and walked down the hall to Hopie's kindergarten room. The hall was lined with paper turkeys and crayon drawings of the Pilgrims and Indians. So was Hope's classroom. But something else was there, too. Christmas. It had started creeping in.

Hope was waiting for us with a grin on her face and a Christmas bell made from a section of an egg carton in her hand.

"Look! Look what we made today!" she cried, running over to us with the bell extended. "A Christmas bell! Just like with Mrs. Harper."

Miss Donnelly smiled at me from her desk. "A great day," she said, meaning that Hopie hadn't cried and had played with the other kids and stuff.

"Good," I said. At least somebody was having a great day.

Hope put her coat and mittens on, and Miss Donnelly handed me a big paper bag full of stuff. "We cleaned out our cubbies today," she explained.

"There was a spider in mine," added Hope. "In the corner. We put him in a jar and watched him, and then we let him go."

"Have a nice Thanksgiving, Hope," Miss Donnelly said as we walked toward the door. "Eat lots of turkey."

Hope giggled. When we were out in the hall she said, "Miss Donnelly is funny."

I glanced at Denise and she smiled. This seemed to be our old Hopie. I was glad she was coming back.

Halfway home, Hope suddenly stopped in her tracks.

"What is it?" I asked.

"Mommy said we could buy decorations for Christmas cookies today, remember?"

I did, vaguely. But I was cold and tired and hungry, and I didn't feel like walking back to the little grocery store near the elementary school. Particularly not for something connected with Christmas.

"We'll get them on Monday, Hope," I told her. "We're

not going to make cookies yet anyway. It's not close enough to Christmas."

Hope pouted. "But Mommy promised."

"We won't be using the stuff for weeks. We'll get the decorations on Monday, okay?"

"No."

"Liza, it'll only take ten minutes to walk back there," Denise pointed out.

I shot her a look usually reserved for Carrie. "Monday, Hope," I said.

Hope began to cry, and Denise stopped talking to me. But when we reached Bayberry, Denise said, "Have a good Thanksgiving, you guys."

"Thanks. You, too.... Have fun at the party."

"Yeah."

"Will you call me on Sunday and tell me all about it?"

"You really want me to?"

I nodded.

"Okay. Sure."

I knew we weren't mad at each other, but something was different between us.

When we got home, Hopie wouldn't shut up about her stupid cookie decorations. She talked about them until bedtime. She told Carrie I was a meanie, she told Mom I was a wicked witch, and she told Brent I was a bullfrog, which was her new word for people she didn't like. (Her doctor was a bullfrog, the cafeteria monitor was a bullfrog...)

Nobody seemed to mind. Even though the next day would be Thanksgiving, they were all talking about Christmas. I felt surrounded by it. Mom and Carrie were planning to go shopping on Saturday. Brent was trying to figure out a budget that would allow enough money for a one-day trip to New York City during December. And Hope began babbling about Santa's Village—in between remarks about people who were bullfrogs.

That night, I went to bed angry. I woke up angry the next morning, I was angry during Thanksgiving at the Werners', and I was angry all weekend, particularly when everybody went off Christmas shopping bright and early on Saturday.

Sunday made me even angrier. Denise called to tell me about Justin's party. She had had a wonderful time and was in love with Justin Sommerville. But she accidentally let slip that Marc had spent almost the entire party talking to Cathryn Lynn.

On Monday I was awakened by Hope. She was standing next to my bed with a look on her face that could only be described as devilish.

"What?" I mumbled.

"Today we're buying cookie decorations. You said so."

What a pill she could be.

"You woke me up for *that?* What if I say no?" I asked her.

For a moment, Hopie looked scared. Then she narrowed her eyes at me. "You won't."

"Why not?"

"Because Mommy *told* you to take me to the store."

"I know."

"Are you going to?"

"Yes."

"I knew it! I knew it!"

"Hope," I said, "you're being a bullfrog. Leave me alone."

That afternoon, Carrie had another art club meeting. I picked Hope up at school and walked her across the street to the little grocery store. Mom had given us five dollars, and Hope chose containers of colored sugar, jimmies, and silver balls, and three tubes of frosting—red, green, and white. I handed her the money and told her she could pay for the stuff herself, which she'd never done before. She looked rather proud as we left the store. We turned to head home and walked by the hardware store next door.

"Oh!" cried Hopie, running to the window and pointing at something inside.

"What is it, Tink?"

"Look at those tools—the ones in that case."

I looked. There was a leather case full of screwdrivers, neatly lined up and arranged according to size.

"If Daddy were here," Hope went on, "I'd buy that for him for Christmas. He'd like that, wouldn't he?"

"Hopie! How can you say that?"

She turned around to stare at me. "What?"

"Dad can never enjoy another Christmas. He'll never get any more presents."

"I know—"

"Don't you see? So nobody else should have presents either. It's just not right. It's unfair to Dad. We shouldn't have presents or Christmas this year."

I started to walk away, leaving Hope by the hardware store. After a few seconds, she ran to catch up with me. She reached for my hand and held it all the way home. Neither of us said a word.

The next day, Carrie picked Hope up, and I got to go home by myself for once. I was sitting in the kitchen enjoying the peace and quiet of a late afternoon in winter when the front door opened and closed. I listened. No voices.

"Carrie?" I called. "Hope? Is that you?"

Carrie came into the kitchen alone. "It's us," she said.

"Where's Hope?"

"Going up to Mom's room. I'm really worried, Liza. Something's wrong. Miss Donnelly gave me a note— a sealed one—to give to Mom tonight. She said there was a little problem at school today. And Hopie wouldn't talk all the way home, except to say she wanted to go to her room."

"Oh, no."

Carrie looked longingly at the note. "I wonder if we could steam—"

I cut her off, shaking my head. "No. Mom would know. We'll just have to wait."

Hope was still upstairs when Mom got home. Carrie didn't even give Mom a chance to take off her coat. She thrust the note at her while she was still standing in front of the closet.

"It's from Miss Donnelly," Carrie informed her. "There's a problem."

Mom looked as if she needed a problem about as much as she needed dandruff. She sighed, hung up her coat, and opened the note right there in the front hall.

"What's it say? What's it say?" Carrie asked.

I hovered behind her. "It must be pretty bad. Hopie's been in your room all afternoon."

"Well," said Mom, "it seems that Hope took the classroom tool kit out of Miss Donnelly's desk today and hid it in her cubby. Apparently, she was going to take it home. Now, why would Hope take a *tool kit*, of all things?"

Tool kit. I began to feel a little funny. Did it have anything to do with yesterday, with what I'd said to her? I shifted from one foot to the other. I couldn't figure out the connection, though. Hopie had wanted the tools for Dad, but she knew very well she couldn't give them to him. She'd said so herself. I decided to keep quiet about the incident at the hardware store. After all, Hope *hadn't* taken the tools. Mom would talk to her about stealing, and everything would be okay.

But Mom didn't talk to her. Instead, she talked to a friend of hers who was a child psychologist. I overheard her on the phone that evening. Mom told her friend she'd decided Hope needed help. She described Hope's behavior lately, ending with the tool-kit incident. Then she asked how much it would cost for Hope to see a doctor once or twice a week. When I heard her repeat "Seventy-five dollars an hour?" I was shocked. I knew I had to talk to her. We couldn't afford that much money. Besides, Hope needed to talk to *me*, not to some doctor.

As soon as she hung up the phone, I told Mom how Hope had seen some tools she would have wanted to give Dad for Christmas if he were still alive. "You know," said Mom, "I never bothered to ask Hope *why* she took the tools. I think we better do that now."

Hope was upstairs with Brent and Carrie. They were telling her stories before she went to bed. Mom shooed them out, then sat me on the bed with Hope.

"Okay," said Mom, pacing the room. "Hope, Liza told me you saw a tool kit in the hardware store yesterday. She said you wanted to buy it for Daddy. Is that right?" Hope nodded.

"Does that have anything to do with why you tried to take Miss Donnelly's tools today? Why did you want Miss Donnelly's tools?"

"Liza said if Daddy couldn't have presents, no one could."

Mom frowned. "But what were you going to do with the tools?"

"Give them to Daddy—at his grave. Liza doesn't know that we really *can* give him presents. She never comes to the graveyard." She turned to me. "See, Liza, we give Daddy flowers all the time. The flowers are presents...aren't they, Mommy?"

"Well, in a way," replied Mom. "So you were going to give Daddy the tools?"

"Yes. And then it would be okay for *us* to get presents. Liza said."

I sighed.

"Oh," said Mom. "I think I see. Liza, would you leave us alone for awhile, please? I want to talk to your sister. Then I want to talk to you."

I went to my room and kicked Carrie out.

"More privacy?" she asked.

"Yeah."

"Boy, I can't wait until Brent goes to college. Then you can have all the privacy you want."

When Mom came in a few minutes later, she sat on my bed looking annoyed. "What did I tell you?" she said.

"I don't—"

"I said you didn't have to participate in Christmas, but that you were not to spoil anything for the others. And I don't ever want you saying things like this to Hope again. Is that clear?"

I nodded.

"She's confused enough as it is. She doesn't need guilt or anything else piled on top of her. Tomorrow I'll have to call Miss Donnelly and explain this to her. And the next time you pick Hope up at school, I want you to apologize to Miss Donnelly."

"Aw, Mom."

"I mean it, Liza. I'm not sure what's going on with you and Christmas and Dad's death, but the rest of us are getting a bit tired of your martyred sensitivity. You're not the only one who lost someone you loved. Your sisters and brother lost their father, too. And I lost my husband. I want you to think about that. And if you feel you'd like to talk to a counselor, let me know. I can arrange it. It might be a good idea for you."

"Okay."

Mom left the room then, and I sat on my bed. I looked at Carrie's messy half of the room and wished again for my old bedroom at 25 Bayberry. I wished for Dad. I wished for life the way it had been a year earlier.

I cried for awhile, and then I tried to do my homework.

Chapter Seven

After Denise told me about Marc and Cathryn Lynn, I was positive I had lost him for good. And sure enough, Marc barely spoke to me during the entire week after Thanksgiving. However, I didn't see him with Cathryn Lynn either. She ate lunch with Denise and Margie and me every day, and she never said a word about either Marc or the party.

"Did they have a good time?" I asked Denise as we walked home from school one day.

"I don't know. I guess so."

"Has Cathryn Lynn mentioned him at all?"

"No."

"Denise?" I said. I felt a rather personal conversation coming on. Denise and I hadn't had one of those since our fight. "I have to talk to you."

"Okay." She smiled at me. "Now? Or do you want to go to my house?"

"Oh, now is fine. It's this thing with Marc," I began.

"I thought so," said Denise.

"I can't explain everything...exactly. It's not that I don't want to. It's because I don't understand all of it myself. But the thing is, I'm having a hard time with Christmas this year. You know how important Christmas was to my dad."

"Yeah," said Denise.

"It's just so hard to have it this year without him." I was leaving out a lot, but this was the only part of the problem I felt like discussing.

"Our first Christmas without my dad was hard, too," said Denise.

"It was?"

"Yeah, real hard. Holidays always are."

"Yeah," I agreed glumly.

"But why didn't you want to go to Justin's party? What does that have to do with Christmas?" asked Denise.

"Oh, I don't know. It's all mixed up."

"I guess this whole season is tough," said Denise thoughtfully. "But you know, there are probably going to be other parties and stuff. What if Marc asks you to something else? If you keep turning him down, you'll lose him forever. It's like cutting off your nose to spite your face."

"I think I've already lost him," I said.

"I wouldn't be too sure."

"Really?" I said excitedly.

"Really."

I felt a lot better.

But what made me feel really terrific was when Marc smiled at me in math class the following day as if nothing had ever happened. Ms. Pressman turned her back to write an equation on the board, and I let my eyes drift toward the windows and the snow that was falling beyond them. But before they reached the windows, they ran into Marc's eyes. And Marc's eyes crinkled as he smiled at me.

I managed to squeeze in a smile of my own before Ms. Pressman turned around again, and the next thing I knew, I was being passed another note.

"Liza—I'm sorry I got mad," this one said. "Meet me on the playground today. Same time, same place. Okay?—Marc."

I nodded at him, grinning, and just managed to wipe the smile off my face before Ms. Pressman turned back to us. Maybe Denise had been right!

That day, I beat Marc to the cement yard. I had finished my lunch in a hurry and had run outdoors to wait for him. He showed up just a few moments later. My heart began to pound. Why did the sight of Marc always make that happen?

"Hi," he said. "If you're cold, we could go back inside."

"No, that's okay. Let's stay out here. I like the snow."

"All right," said Marc. And then, "Well...I'm not sure why you haven't wanted to do anything with me yet. I mean, I'm not saying you're lying, but, like, I have this feeling you could have gone to the movies or the party but you—you—I don't know."

"Oh, Marc. I can't explain—"

"Look, I know your father died and all. Maybe that has something to do with it, but anyway, I want to ask you out one more time."

One more time. It sounded like a last chance.

"Next weekend Carlo Giannelli is having a Christmas party. I want you to come with me. It's Friday at six o'clock."

I drew in a deep breath. "I think I can come. I do have to check with Mom, but I think I can come." The words just popped out of my mouth. I couldn't believe I'd just said them. I hated parties, and I didn't want anything to do with Christmas or having fun, yet there I was telling Marc I'd go to Carlo's Christmas party.

I didn't want to lose Marc.

That evening, I talked to Mom in private in her bedroom. I told her about the party and asked if I could go. "I don't need any new clothes," I told her.

"Who asked you to this party?" said Mom.

"Marc Radlay."

"Isn't he the boy who broke your other date?"

"Mom," I said, "I lied. I didn't want to go to the movies with him. It's hard to explain. I was just afraid. But I'm going to go to this party. If I don't, I'll never get to do anything with Marc."

"Liza," Mom said. She sat me next to her on Hope's side of the double bed. "What were you afraid of?"

"I can't explain it, Mom."

"Are you afraid of boys?"

"Oh, no. Not that. It's completely different."

"Could you please try to explain? I'd really like to understand."

I didn't say anything.

"Does it have to do with Dad?" Mom asked.

"Sort of."

"Well, I can't force you to tell me what's bothering you, but I also can't help you if you don't."

"I know."

Mom sighed. "If you ever do want to talk about it," she said at last, "I'm here. I hope you know that."

"I do. Thanks, Mom."

We hugged each other, and then Hope came in and we put her to bed.

"I can go," I told Marc the next day. I didn't even wait to meet him in the cement yard. I caught him right after math class.

"Really?" said Marc. This huge grin spread across his face. "That's great!" He turned and walked down the hall.

The party was nine days away. In those nine days I fixed my hair about twenty different ways and tried on at least a million outfits. I tried on all my jewelry, and I fooled around with the makeup Denise had given me.

By Friday at five I was a wreck, but I chose an outfit anyway. I decided on jeans, a funky pink sweat shirt, and barrettes with long streamers to wear in my hair.

When I was finished and standing in front of Mom's full-length mirror, I had to admit I looked very nice. Maybe even pretty.

I called Denise to see how she was doing. She and Justin were both going to be at the party.

"Hi," I said when she picked up the phone. "Are you ready?"

"I'm going crazy!" she cried. "You know my new blue pants?"

"Yeah."

"Those are what I'm wearing, but then I couldn't decide whether to put on the striped sweater or the sweat shirt with the sheep on it."

"Wear the sweat shirt," I said.

"Well, I was going to, but I tried it on so many times I got a hole in it."

"Oh!" I couldn't help giggling. Then I added, "I'm so nervous. Promise me something."

"What?"

"If you see me standing around alone, come talk to me, okay?"

"Okay, but I can promise you something else—I won't have to. Marc is so wild about you, he won't leave you for a second."

"Really? I mean, he really likes me that much?"

"Trust me."

At ten minutes to six, the doorbell rang and there was Marc standing on our front steps. His mother was sitting in the car in our driveway.

"Hi, Marc. Come on in," said Mom warmly.

"Mom, we have to *go*," I said.

"Oh, hang on. I just want to see the two of you together."

Marc was blushing furiously.

"Mo-*ther*," I said. This was so embarrassing. After all, Marc was just picking me up. It wasn't as if he were my *date* or something.

"Oh, all right," said Mom. "Have fun."

"Okay," I said. I waved to her and we ran out the front door.

Marc's mother drove us to the Giannellis'.

"My Mom'll pick us up," I told Mrs. Radlay as I was getting out of the car. "She said she'd come by at ten."

"That's fine," replied Marc's mother. "Have fun, kids."

Fun. Right. Marc couldn't possibly know how much I didn't want to do this.

But when he reached for my hand while we were waiting for someone to answer the door and said, "You look really nice, Liza," I felt a lot better.

Carlo's father answered the door and showed us the room where we could leave our coats.

"Ready?" asked Marc.

"Sure," I said.

For a few exciting seconds we gazed into one another's eyes.

Then we heard Mr. Giannelli letting Justin and Denise in. When they had taken off their coats, we went into the rec room. The Giannellis had decorated it for

Christmas. Red and green cloths covered the tables where food had been set out. A little Christmas tree stood in one corner. Streamers crisscrossed the ceiling and colored lights outlined the doorway to the front hall.

"Come on, let's get some food," said Marc. He steered me toward one of the tables.

And that was the beginning of one of the longest evenings of my life.

Denise was right. Marc barely left me alone for a second. The time passed quickly. It was about two hours later, after we'd eaten and talked and danced to loud music, when someone said, "Let's sing Christmas carols!"

Several boys groaned, but all the girls thought it was a good idea, even Denise, who knew she would have to play the piano.

We went into the Giannellis' living room. Denise sat on the piano bench.

"Do you need music?" asked Carlo.

"No," said Denise. "Not as long as we stick to carols everybody knows."

So we gathered around Denise, and someone called out, "'The First Noel'!" And we began singing. It was when we were in the middle of "Hark, the Herald Angels Sing" that I suddenly had to stop. One minute, I was around the piano with all those kids, and the next, I was remembering a snowy afternoon last Christmas when our family had sung carols by the fire. I remembered it as if it were yesterday and all those days between had never passed.

To my horror, I felt my eyes fill with tears, but I was *not* going to cry in the middle of Carlo Giannelli's Christmas party. I made a dash for the bathroom, couldn't find it, and ended up in the room where we'd put our coats. But I hadn't been there for more than ten seconds when the door opened and Marc came in.

"Liza! What's the matter?" he said.

Do not cry, I told myself sternly. "It was just that carol. It made me think of my dad....I want to go home. Do you know where the Giannellis' phone is?"

"Do you *have* to go? I think they're getting tired of singing."

"I shouldn't have come here in the first place," I told Marc.

"What do you mean? Why not? Your mother said it was all right."

"It's not that. It's just...it's not right for me to have fun when my Dad is...when my Dad can't. I'm not even going to celebrate Christmas this year."

Marc looked terribly embarrassed, as if he'd rather be anywhere except here talking about my dead father. But he said, "Don't you think your dad would want you to enjoy yourself?"

"Oh, that's what everyone says, but it just doesn't feel right."

"Do you feel better *not* having fun?" Marc asked me incredulously.

"I don't know...."

Marc cleared a space on the couch, and we sat down

next to the mountain of coats. His red face was starting to return to its regular color.

"Are you happy now?" he asked.

"*No!*" I snapped. "My father's dead. How could I be happy?"

"I don't know. I mean—" Marc's face was blazing again. "So you're going to forget Christmas this year? I bet your dad wouldn't like that. I mean, unless he was really selfish or something."

I jumped up. "My father was not selfish! He was very generous. He wanted everyone to enjoy Christmas because he liked it so much. He—ohhhh," I said. I sat down again. "I guess my father wouldn't *exactly* approve of what I'm doing. *I'm* the one who's being selfish. I'm sorry I yelled at you."

"That's all right. ... Well..." Marc looked around uncomfortably. "You want to go back to the party now? We can't stay in here all night. If anyone found out, they'd think we were ... you know..."

I giggled, then stopped abruptly. "I can't go back."

"What are you going to do instead? Do you still want to go home?"

"I guess not. But I can't sing carols anymore. I just can't."

"Okay," said Marc. "Hey, listen."

"What? I don't hear anything."

"I know. That's what I mean."

And at that moment, a Bruce Springsteen song came blaring out of the tape deck.

"Come on," said Marc. "You can go back now, can't you?"

I giggled again. "Okay, let's go." I felt as if a weight had been lifted from my chest.

But the evening wasn't over yet. When I finally crawled into bed a couple of hours later, I'd been lying there for only a few seconds, thinking of Marc and the party, when I became aware of little sniffing noises and muffled sounds coming from Carrie's bed.

I flicked on my reading light and saw Carrie lying in a rumpled mess of blankets with her pillow over her head. "Hey, what's wrong?" I asked her. "Did you get in trouble?"

"No." Her voice sounded very small.

"Why are you crying?"

"I just miss Dad, that's all."

"You do?"

Carrie didn't answer.

"You really miss him?"

"Leave me alone."

"But I thought you didn't care."

Carrie yanked the pillow from her face and slammed it on her bed. "You thought I didn't *care?*"

"Shh!" I said. "Mom'll come in."

"Well, what made you think that? You're the one who won't go to the cemetery."

"But you didn't do anything about his birthday, and

you're all caught up in the art club and baby-sitting and—"

"It doesn't mean I've forgotten. I think about him all the time. I'm lonely and I miss him, okay? Are you happy? Now let me go to sleep."

"Carrie, I'm sorry. I didn't understand. But I'm trying to now."

"That's okay," she said.

"If you want to talk about Dad sometime, we can."

"Okay. Thanks."

"Good night."

"Good night, Liza."

Chapter Eight

The next morning I woke up feeling like Scrooge— not like the "Bah! Humbug" Scrooge, but like the Scrooge who awakens after he's been visited by the three spirits and realizes he hasn't missed Christmas after all, and now he has only a few hours to dress and buy a turkey and do all his shopping.

I looked at the calendar on my desk. There were about three weeks until Christmas. I had an awful lot to do. I knew it would be hard, but I could always change my mind again.

In her bed, Carrie moaned, rolled over, yawned, and opened one eye.

"Hi," I said to the eye. "Want to go Christmas shopping today?"

The eye closed. "Phlmrstrp." Then both eyes opened. "*Christmas* shopping?" she said.

"Don't ask. Do you want to go or not?"

"Well, sure. I've got a lot left to do."

"Okay. Maybe someone will drive us to the mall."
After all, I thought, if I got there and couldn't go through
with it, Carrie and I could always go to a movie or get
a hamburger. I hadn't seen much of her lately anyway.

So later that morning, Mom dropped us off. She didn't
ask any questions. When Carrie had told her we were
going Christmas shopping, she had raised an eyebrow,
and that was it.

Neither Carrie nor I had nearly as much money to
spend as we'd had last year because we weren't allowed to dip into our savings accounts, but we had our
allowances, and Carrie had her baby-sitting money,
and I had some birthday money left over.

So we went to the stores and did our Christmas shopping. Then we ate lunch at Friendly's. And after that,
we stood by Barton's Men's Store, waiting for Mom to
pick us up. I was looking idly in the window at the
suits and ties and belts when something occurred to
me. I knew I was going to have to call Denise as soon
as I got home.

"Denise," I said. I was standing in our kitchen with
my coat on, still holding the packages from the mall.
"Can I come over? I have to ask you something."

"Sure," she said. "Come right now."

I hid the stuff I'd bought under my bed and dashed
over to Denise's. It took a little longer to get there than
it had when we lived at 25 Bayberry, but soon I was
sitting across from her on her bed, hugging a pillow.
Denise was setting a bowl of M&M's between us.

"So?" she said.

"So I realized something while Carrie and I were out shopping today."

"What?"

"We have to get Marc and Justin Christmas presents. I mean, don't we?" I figured that of all people, I should give Marc a present.

Denise's hand, which was on its way to her mouth full of M&M's, stopped in midair. "Oh, wow! You're right. I guess we do."

"What do you get for a boy?"

"Well, what do you get Brent?" Denise countered.

"Oh, forget that. Brother stuff—socks or underwear, or things he's asked for. But we can't get Marc and Justin socks or underwear. And they haven't asked for anything. And we can't afford really nice gifts, like sweaters."

Denise put the handful of M&M's in her mouth and thought. She put another handful in and thought some more.

"Maybe," I said, "we could get them something meaningful."

"Yeah? Like what?"

"Like if Justin has a favorite song, you could get him the tape it's on. Something like that."

"Oh, that's a good idea."

"We'll have to think."

"Yeah."

That evening at dinner, Brent, our very own household budget analyst, said, "I don't see how we can afford that trip to New York I was thinking about and do everything else for Christmas that we've planned."

"No," said Mom. "I agree. New York is out. I don't think we have a free Saturday before Christmas anyway."

"But," said Brent, "even though it's expensive, maybe we could still go out to Thompson's to chop down a tree, instead of just buying a cut one here in town."

"I guess so," Mom replied. "Sure. That's a good idea."

"Could we go tomorrow?" asked Brent.

"Yeah, please?" cried Carrie.

"Please, please, please?" chimed in Hope.

"Why not?" said Mom. "Liza, do you want to come with us?"

I wasn't sure I did, but I said I would anyway. I figured I could always stay in the car, if necessary.

But I had a feeling it might not be necessary. Just before dinner, one of Mom's friends had dropped by and smoked three cigarettes. After she'd left, Mom had asked me to empty the ashtray. It wasn't until twenty minutes later that I remembered about "flakes of Dad." And when I did remember, I smiled. It seemed silly now. Besides, I had so many other things to think about—like Marc—that I didn't have time to remember "flakes of Dad" every time I saw an ash.

"Yay!" shouted Hopie. "Liza's coming!"

"Maybe," I said.

The next day we piled into the car and Brent drove

us out to Thompson's. When we arrived, Mom got out and looked around.

"Your father really used to love this place," she said. "He came here for a Christmas tree every year from the time he was thirteen."

"My age," I said.

Mom nodded.

"Do you think he'd be glad we came here without him this year?" I asked anxiously.

"I don't think he'd have wanted it any other way. We can carry on the tradition for him," replied Mom. "Brent, this was a good idea."

We chose a fat little tree and took it home with us. Everyone really got into the spirit then and brought some of the decorations out of the attic. But I'd had enough, and I sat down in the kitchen to do some homework. I didn't want to see the tree or the decorations.

The phone rang.

I answered it. "Hello?"

"Hello, is Liza there?"

"This is Liza."

"Hi. It's Marc."

"Hi!" I cried.

"Would you like to—If you don't want to, I'll understand. It'll be okay. But next Saturday, a bunch of kids from our class are going Christmas caroling. Justin and Denise are going, and Margie and Cathryn Lynn and Carlo and about six others. Then we're going to Tommy Schwartz's for hot chocolate and stuff. I'm sure we

wouldn't have to sing "Hark, the Herald Angels Sing."
Want to go with me?"

I paused. "Sure...," I said slowly. "Yeah, I guess so.
Let me check with Mom. Hold on."

I got Mom out of the living room, where she was
looking through a big box of tree ornaments.

"Marc wants to know if I can go Christmas caroling
with some kids next Saturday. Denise is going."

"Of course," said Mom. She looked at me thoughtfully. "Are you afraid?"

"Yes," I admitted, "but I'm still going to go."

Mom kissed me on the forehead. "I love you," she
said.

I returned to the phone and gave Marc the good
news.

Saturday morning arrived with snow. It snowed all
day and was still snowing at dinnertime, but we decided to go caroling anyway. I bundled up in layers of
clothes and walked to Denise's house. Then Mrs. Petersen drove us slowly through the silent white streets
to Tommy's house, where the carolers were meeting.

Tommy handed out little songbooks, and we started
walking through his neighborhood, singing at each
home. Everywhere we went, people came to their front
doors to listen and to offer us cookies or chocolates.

I think we were at the sixth house when Marc took
my hand. I couldn't feel it too well since we were each
wearing two pairs of mittens, so that there were four
layers of wool between my hand and his, but it didn't
matter.

We held hands until we returned to Tommy's house an hour later. And just before everyone's parents started arriving, Marc kissed me quickly on the cheek. "Merry Christmas, Liza," he said.

At first the words froze on my lips, but at last I got them out. "Merry Christmas," I whispered.

I went home in a daze.

The next day, I couldn't think of anything but Marc. He was everywhere. I floated through the morning.

After lunch, Mom said, "Liza? Carrie and Hope and I are going to the cemetery this afternoon. Would you like to come with us?"

I knew what she was thinking. I was changing, calming down. I was going to take part in Christmas, maybe. I had other things on my mind besides Dad. (Marc, for instance.) But I could not face that cemetery yet. The cemetery was Dad dead, just like the ashes were. And I didn't want to deal with it.

I shook my head. "I don't think so," I told Mom. "Not yet."

Chapter Nine

Buying Marc's Christmas present started out as a little project and turned into a gigantic one. I could not think of anything to give him that was both meaningful and cheap. Denise was having as much trouble as I was.

We didn't know what the boys' favorite songs were. We couldn't afford sweaters or tie clips or cuff links. Scarves were boring.

Something meaningful, I kept telling myself.

Finally there were just five shopping days left until Christmas. Denise and I were frantic.

"What does Justin like?" I asked Denise for the eighty-seventh time.

"I've told you," she said. "Ships and sailing. And old Beatles albums.... And I don't *know* which old Beatles albums he already has," she said when she realized I was about to suggest getting him one.

I sighed, said good night, and hung up the phone.

That night I thought of a truly great present for Marc. The idea came to me in a dream. The next morning, I called Denise before I'd even eaten breakfast. "I know what to get Marc!" I exclaimed. "Come shopping with me after school today, okay?"

When school let out, Denise and I picked up Hopie, who was brimming over with smiles and art projects. "Look!" she cried, running across her classroom to meet us. "A macaroni chain! It's better than the old one, the one I made at my other school. This one has *sparkles*." Hopie turned to smile adoringly at Miss Donnelly, the provider of the sparkles, and Miss Donnelly smiled at Hopie, then at me.

Hopie had been having one good day after another since we got the tool-kit business straightened out. And Miss Donnelly had been very nice when I apologized to her.

"Okay, Sissy, let's go," I said. "We have one little Christmas present to buy before we go home."

With the help of Denise, Miss Donnelly, and me, Hopie got dressed in her sweater, parka, snow pants, hat, mittens, extra socks, and boots, and waddled out the door.

"Where are we going?" she asked.

"To Look Again."

"Look Again?" repeated Denise. "The used-book store?"

"Yup."

At Look Again, which was a cramped, musty-smelling place with wall after wall of old, dusty books, I headed

right for the D shelf in the fiction section and found
exactly what I wanted. In fact, I found three of them—
old copies of Charles Dickens's *A Christmas Carol*.

"*A Christmas Carol*?" asked Denise.

"To remind him of the beginning of...us. Because
the play was sort of the beginning. I mean, I already
liked him, but he didn't know *me* until then."

I looked through the books. Because they were used,
they were cheap, but they were old and interesting. I
chose one that had slick color pictures inside, and then
took Hopie to look at the children's books.

She was leafing through a dog-eared copy of *The
Cat in the Hat* when Denise suddenly shouted, "I've
got it! I've found the present for Justin!"

She ran over to us carrying an old print of a sailing
ship. The print was yellowed and curling, but the ship
was magnificent with its masts and sails.

"I can mount it for him," said Denise. "Then it will
look better. He can hang it on his bedroom wall."

So Denise bought the ship print for Justin, and I
bought the Dickens book for Marc and *The Cat in the
Hat* for Hopie, who was very close to being able to
read it herself. Then we walked home, feeling elated.

Two days later, school was out. And two days after
that was Christmas Eve. I had invited Marc over for
dinner, but he couldn't make it because his family was
going out to eat. However, he was coming over at five-
thirty so we could exchange gifts.

At four forty-five I was sitting alone in the living

room, which was unusual in the new little house. Mom was doing something behind closed doors in the den, Carrie was helping Hope to wrap her Christmas presents in our bedroom, and Brent was at Ellen's house.

The living room was warm and Christmasy and smelled good. The tree was still fresh, and we had put sprigs of holly and yew branches on the mantlepiece. A stout red bayberry candle was burning on the coffee table. The dark room glowed with firelight, candlelight, and the tree lights. I had turned all the lamps off.

Beneath the tree were a few presents from friends and neighbors, but our family presents were hidden away under beds and in the dark depths of closets. Hopie still believed in Santa Claus. That was the last year she was a believer. That night our family would put out cookies for Santa, and listen for sleigh bells or reindeer hooves on the roof, and check the sky for magical sights.

I curled up on one end of the couch and enjoyed the warmth and peacefulness of the room. The only sounds were the logs snapping and crackling in the fireplace and the distant strains of Christmas carols from the radio Mom had with her in the den. I closed my eyes and pretended I was at 25 Bayberry. I could almost transport myself back to other times.

I pretended Dad was sitting next to me. He was drinking a glass of eggnog and telling me about Christmas in New York City. When I opened my eyes again, I felt impossibly sad. That had been too real.

I began to cry. I put my hands over my eyes and sobbed silently. I cried and cried and couldn't stop, and even though the crying hurt terribly, I could feel some of the misery draining away.

Then I started to worry about Marc. I didn't want to look too hideous when he got here. I kept checking my watch. At twenty minutes after five, I stood up, wiped my eyes, and went into the bathroom to wash my face. Then I put on some makeup. I didn't look too bad.

The doorbell rang as I was zipping up the makeup case. I ran to answer it. "Hi!" I said to Marc. "Come on inside."

Marc stepped into the front hall, brushing at his jacket. A light snow had just begun to fall. He took off his jacket, and I saw that underneath he was wearing a gray suit. He looked very handsome.

"Merry Christmas," he said. "Mom just dropped me off. She's going to pick me up in half an hour."

"Okay," I replied. "Do you want anything to drink? Do you like eggnog?"

Marc made a face, so I got Cokes for us instead.

We sat in the living room. I hoped everyone would stay where they were so Marc and I could be alone together.

"Your tree is nice," Marc said.

"Thanks. We always go out to Thompson's to chop one down."

"You do? So do we!"

I knelt to take a red and green package from under the tree. "Here. This is for you."

"Thanks," said Marc. He pulled a small silver box out of the pocket of his jacket. "And this is for you."

We smiled nervously at one another. Suddenly, I felt shy. "Open yours first," I said.

Marc tore away the wrapping. "*A Christmas Carol!*" Thanks, Liza. This is great." Marc grinned. "Now open yours."

I held the silver box in my hands for a moment, just looking at it. I wanted to remember it. Then I carefully lifted the lid. Inside was a thin silver bracelet. A note was attached to it. I glanced at Marc, then opened the note, which was written on a folded piece of notebook paper, just like the kind he sent me in Ms. Pressman's class. The note read:

> *Wear this and think of me.*
> *Love, Marc.*

"Oh, I will," I said. "Here. Can you put it on my wrist?"

Marc fastened the bracelet. Then he leaned forward and kissed me gently.

A car horn sounded outside.

"That's Mom," said Marc. "I have to go."

My lips were tingling. "Already?"

"Yeah. We have reservations. I'll call you tomorrow. Merry Christmas!"

* * *

Later than evening, the O'Hara family gathered in the living room. The O'Hara family. I guessed we could still call ourselves that.

I was going to celebrate Christmas after all, but with a lot less enthusiasm than usual. At the time, Marc seemed more important than Christmas.

Christmas or not, I was feeling warm and cozy. The fire was going, our stockings were hung, and Hopie was holding *The Night Before Christmas* in her lap, but she had other, more important things on her mind.

"How can Santa come down the chimney if there's a fire in the fireplace?" she asked.

Mom squirmed. "Because he's magic, honey."

"How does his pack fit down the chimney? And how can Santa fit enough presents for all the children in the world in one pack?"

Hope had an awful lot of questions this year, and they were more logical than the ones she used to ask. It was the beginning of the end of believing.

Then Hope changed the subject. "Okay, let's read." She patted the book. "Who will read it?"

Good question. There was no more Dad.

"Who do you want to read it?" Mom asked her.

Hope looked pained. Then she giggled. "Fifi," she said and stuck the book between Fifi's huge paws.

Fifi sniffed at it.

We laughed.

Then Hope handed the book to me. "I want Liza to read it."

"Me?" Oh, no....

Hope crawled across Brent and plopped herself in my lap. I settled back, trying to relax, the scent of Hope's freshly shampooed hair filling my nose. Next to me, wedged between my leg and the arm of the couch, Mouse dozed. On my other side were Brent and Fifi. Carrie sat at my feet playing with Dr. J. Across the room, Mom was curled up in an armchair.

I took a deep breath, then opened the book.

"'Twas the night before Christmas," I began, "and all through the house, not a creature was stirring, not even a..."

"Mouse!" Hopie supplied.

"The stockings were hung by the chimney with care..."

I heard my voice reading on, and for a second—just a second—I was positive that Dad was in the room with us, somewhere, enjoying our Christmas. It was a very comforting feeling.

Later, when we were going to bed, Mom leaned over to kiss me good night, and I said, "When are you going to the cemetery again?"

"Tomorrow afternoon, sweetheart. Why?"

"I think I'll go with you."

Epilogue

We survived Christmas.

We survived winter.

And that spring, good things happened for all of us. Mom was accepted into a special program at the community college, where she could take business courses as well as her courses in educational administration. She said that in a couple of years she'd be qualified for a really top-flight job and could help out much more with college tuitions.

Brent took Ellen Myers to his senior prom. He graduated from Neuport High as the valedictorian of his class, and he was granted a full scholarship to Princeton University. I added an off-center picture of him in his cap and gown to the special photo album I kept under my phone.

Carrie suffered through Ms. Saunders and was promoted to the seventh grade. She got Mr. Landi for

English class. More important, she developed her first crush on a boy—Joshua Sommerville, Justin's younger brother.

Hopie lost her front tooth, taught herself to read, and made a best friend. By the end of the year, she was doing so well that Miss Donnelly sent her home with a special report card, suggesting that Hopie skip first grade. But Mom said no. Hope was smart, but she didn't need any more changes, and she did need to be with children her own age.

And I wound up eighth grade with straight A's and steeled myself to enter high school. Denise and Justin stopped hanging out together, but Marc took me to our graduation dance. We danced all evening and promised to see each other every single day of the long, hot summer ahead.

Two days after that, I visited the cemetery for the first time that summer. I threw out all the dead flowers around Dad's grave and replaced them with stalks of gladioluses from our garden and a handful of dandelions from Hope. Then I sat by Dad's stone and brought him up to date.

"It's been more than a year now," I reminded him. "I'm starting high school in September. Brent got into Princeton. I guess you know all that."

I thought for a moment. "It was a long time before I could talk to you like this. I thought I'd never be able to do it. But now I can. When you were with us, I couldn't imagine what it would feel like to be without you. And when you were first gone, it was so horrible

I couldn't deal with your grave or anything. But now that I can talk to you, I feel like you're with us again. I wonder if I'll always feel that. With you, without you. With you and without you. I don't know the answer, Dad, but the love will always be there."

About the Author

ANN M. MARTIN grew up in Princeton, New Jersey, and is a graduate of Smith College. Her Apple paperbacks are *Yours Turly, Shirley; Ten Kids, No Pets; With You and Without You; Me and Katie (the Pest); Stage Fright; Inside Out; Bummer Summer;* and the books in THE BABY-SITTERS CLUB series and the BABY-SITTERS LITTLE SISTER series.

Ms. Martin lives in New York City with her cat, Mouse. She likes ice cream and *I Love Lucy;* and she hates to cook.

APPLE® PAPERBACKS

ANN M. MARTIN
author of your favorite series

Don't miss any of these
great Apple ® Paperbacks

❑ MW43622-8	**Bummer Summer**	**$2.95**
❑ MW43621-X	**Inside Out**	**$2.75**
❑ MW43828-X	**Ma and Pa Dracula**	**$2.95**
❑ MW43618-X	**Me and Katie (the Pest)**	**$2.75**
❑ MW43619-8	**Stage Fright**	**$2.75**
❑ MW43620-1	**Ten Kids, No Pets**	**$2.75**
❑ MW43625-2	**With You and Without You**	**$2.75**
❑ MW42809-8	**Yours Turly, Shirley**	**$2.75**

Available wherever you buy books...
or use this order form.

Scholastic Inc., P.O. Box 7502, 2931 East McCarty Street, Jefferson City, MO 65102

Please send me the books I have checked above. I am enclosing $_____ (please add
$2.00 to cover shipping and handling). Send check or money order — no cash or
C.O.D.s please.

Name _____

Address _____

City _____ State/Zip _____

Please allow four to six weeks for delivery. Offer good in the U.S. only. Sorry, mail orders are not available to
residents of Canada. Prices subject to change.

AM991

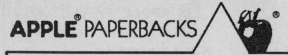

APPLE® PAPERBACKS

Pick an Apple and Polish Off Some Great Reading!

BEST-SELLING APPLE TITLES

❑ MT43944-8	**Afternoon of the Elves** Janet Taylor Lisle	**$2.75**
❑ MT43109-9	**Boys Are Yucko** Anna Grossnickle Hines	**$2.75**
❑ MT43473-X	**The Broccoli Tapes** Jan Slepian	**$2.95**
❑ MT42709-1	**Christina's Ghost** Betty Ren Wright	**$2.75**
❑ MT43461-6	**The Dollhouse Murders** Betty Ren Wright	**$2.75**
❑ MT43444-6	**Ghosts Beneath Our Feet** Betty Ren Wright	**$2.75**
❑ MT44351-8	**Help! I'm a Prisoner in the Library** Eth Clifford	**$2.75**
❑ MT44567-7	**Leah's Song** Eth Clifford	**$2.75**
❑ MT43618-X	**Me and Katie (The Pest)** Ann M. Martin	**$2.75**
❑ MT41529-8	**My Sister, The Creep** Candice F. Ransom	**$2.75**
❑ MT42883-7	**Sixth Grade Can Really Kill You** Barthe DeClements	**$2.75**
❑ MT40409-1	**Sixth Grade Secrets** Louis Sachar	**$2.75**
❑ MT42882-9	**Sixth Grade Sleepover** Eve Bunting	**$2.75**
❑ MT41732-0	**Too Many Murphys** Colleen O'Shaughnessy McKenna	**$2.75**

Available wherever you buy books, or use this order form.

- -

Scholastic Inc., P.O. Box 7502, 2931 East McCarty Street, Jefferson City, MO 65102

Please send me the books I have checked above. I am enclosing $_____ (please add $2.00 to cover shipping and handling). Send check or money order — no cash or C.O.D.s please.

Name _____

Address _____

City_____ State/Zip _____

Please allow four to six weeks for delivery. Offer good in the U.S.A. only. Sorry, mail orders are not available to residents of Canada. Prices subject to change.

APP591